NO
GOOD DEED

BY

PHIL M. WILLIAMS

Phil W Books.
www.PhilWBooks.com

ISBN: 978-1-943894-86-4

A NOTE FROM PHIL

Dear Reader,

If you're interested in receiving **two of my novels for free** and/or reading many of my other titles for free or discounted, go to the following link: http://www.PhilWBooks.com.

You're probably thinking, *What's the catch?* There is no catch.

Sincerely,

Phil M. Williams

CHAPTER 1: LIZZIE AND THE SHORE

The two married couples sat around the dining room table, the chandelier overhead providing warm light. Hutches ran along the east and west walls, displaying ornate china. Lizzie and Brad sipped their drinks—wine for her and whisky for him. Dennis and Julie sat across the table from them, doing the same.

"You two should come with us to the shore this summer," Julie said. "Dennis's brother can't make it, so we'll have two extra rooms."

Lizzie touched Brad's hand. "We'd love that. I need to get into bathing-suit shape though."

"I doubt that. You look great," Dennis replied, from across the table, his gaze locked on Lizzie's cleavage long enough not to be accidental.

Brad tensed, his hand balling into a fist.

Lizzie squeezed his fist, telling him to let it go with her touch, yet feeling butterflies in her stomach.

"I'm the one who needs to get into bathing-suit shape," Julie said.

Dennis glanced at his wife, but he didn't disagree.

"That's ridiculous. *You* look great. Especially …" Lizzie trailed off. She almost said, *especially for your age.*

Julie was forty-two, twelve years older than Lizzie. Julie's age had been a sore spot ever since they'd become friends ten years ago, three years after Brad joined the Carville Police Department. Dennis and Julie had been trying to have a child. Julie thought that she'd missed her window, that her eggs were too old.

Julie frowned. "I need to tighten things up a bit."

When she was younger, Julie was tall and curvy in all the right places, like an Italian Marilyn Monroe, the extra cushion only enhancing her sex appeal. As she aged, her assets had sagged, along with her chances of getting pregnant. Now she wore Spanx and heavy makeup to maintain the illusion of fertility.

1

Dennis tapped his thick midsection, full of steak and potatoes. "We could both use some tightening."

Dennis, or Chief Rhodes as he was known everywhere, resembled Barney Rubble, with his blockhead and stocky frame. Julie often referred to him as a caveman, especially when he forgot their anniversary, came home stinking of booze, or blew up the bathroom after a hearty meal. She always finished her complaint with *but he's my caveman.*

"Thank you for the offer," Brad said, glancing at Lizzie, then addressing the couple across the table, "but the Outer Banks is a little out of our price range."

Over the years, Lizzie had often heard Julie rave about their vacations in Duck, North Carolina, and Brad had heard Lizzie lobby for their own Outer Banks vacation, based on Julie's recommendations. Brad's answer was always no.

"Oh, we would cover the house," Julie said, looking to her husband for confirmation.

Dennis nodded. "We're already getting the house. We have the extra rooms."

Brad showed his palms. "That's nice of you both, but I don't feel right about not payin'."

Lizzie said, "We have a little savings—"

"*No.*"

Lizzie bowed her head, chastened.

Julie raised her eyebrows.

Brad set his cloth napkin on the table and stood. "We should go. I have to work early tomorrow."

***

Brad drove their old Ford Explorer past farms and forest. He hadn't said a word since they left the dinner party. Lizzie peered through the window, thinking about sunbathing at the shore, watching the kids play in the sand. She tried to remember the last time they'd been on vacation. *That shitty cabin in the Poconos. Four years ago.*

Lizzie turned from the window to her husband, hoping he'd cooled. He gripped the steering wheel, his knuckles white, his jaw clenched. A shadow passed over his shaved head. The guys at the police department called him Rogan because he looked like a younger version of the famous podcaster, and there was another Officer Lambert: no relation. He didn't respond to her gaze, so she turned back to the window.

Brad parked in the driveway of their redbrick rambler, next to Helen's Ford Focus. Helen was Lizzie's mother and babysitter for the evening.

Brad pulled the parking brake unnecessarily hard. Lizzie opened the passenger door.

"Where do you think you're goin'?" Brad asked.

Lizzie shut the door, already cowering. "My mother's probably ready to go home."

His lips curled into a sneer. "She can wait."

"Let's not do this. I'm really tired."

"You're *always* tired. I'm the one workin' my ass off, but I have to listen to how *you're* tired."

Lizzie dipped her head. "You're right. I'm sorry."

"Fuck your sorry. You should be sorry for flirtin' with that fuckin' jagoff."

Her voice went up an octave, as she said, "I wasn't flirting with anyone."

Brad reached out with the speed of a viper, grabbing Lizzie by the throat, squeezing. He spoke through gritted teeth. "He was starin' at your tits all night."

Her eyes bulged. Her breath was constricted, causing wheezy inhalations. But she didn't resist.

"I fuckin' told you not to wear that dress, but you don't listen. It puts me in a fucked-up situation. What the hell am I supposed to do? Punch my boss in the face?"

He shoved her by the neck, the side of her head hitting the passenger door glass.

Lizzie gasped for breath and rubbed her head.

He leered at her, one side of his mouth raised in contempt.

"I'm sorry," she said barely above a whisper.

Brad pointed at her. "Another thing. No way in hell we're goin' to the shore with them." He exited their SUV, slamming the door behind him.

Lizzie watched him stalk up the driveway, transforming into the respectable husband and father for Helen's benefit. *He'll probably make some smart-ass comment to my mom about me drinking too much. Then she'll come out to the car and lecture me about being more responsible, about how lucky I am to have such a wonderful husband.*

She closed her eyes and thought about having sex with Dennis, the ultimate passive-aggressive *fuck you* to Brad. She imagined his hulking frame crushing her, sweat on his brow, grunting like an animal. It wasn't the first time she'd fantasized about Dennis.

In fact, she'd fantasized about him for years.

Chapter 2: Luke and the CSA

Luke drilled a skinny hole into the soft soil of the row, using a handheld drill and auger. Dim light came from the nearby greenhouse and the moon. He drilled the holes exactly twenty-four inches apart, moving down the row rapidly. After his hundredth hole, he walked back to the start of the row.

Then he dropped the leggy tomato transplants into the holes, purposely planting them deep to help establish a strong tap root. As he went, he periodically stopped to stretch his aching back. At 6'5", he found bending over took its toll.

Two hours later, he planted the final tomato, stood, and stretched again. He turned on the drip irrigation to give them an initial soaking. He staggered to the house, taking off his dirty gloves. On the doorstep to his old farmhouse, he took off his boots and set his gloves on top.

Luke opened the screen door and stepped inside. The kitchen and nearby dining room were covered in cardboard boxes and produce. Mary stood by the kitchen table, packing boxes of produce for their CSA members. Each week, they prepared a box of fruits and vegetables for their subscribing members, to be delivered to various localities for pickup.

"How's it going?" Luke asked.

Mary set a cluster of beet greens into a cardboard box labeled Archer Farms, looked up at her husband, and smiled. Her green eyes were a little bloodshot, and her braided ponytail was half undone, but she looked beautiful. Luke stepped closer, but she stopped him with her hand.

"You need washed," she said.

He bent over and kissed his wife on the lips. It was an effort for both of them, as he was fifteen inches taller than her but well worth it.

When they separated, he said, "Tomatoes are in the ground."

"Tired?"

Luke nodded. "It's a good tired. How's Abby? She go down okay?"

Abby was their four-month-old.

"Snug as a bug in a rug," Mary replied.

"I can finish the boxes, if you're tired."

She smiled again. "Wash your hands, and we'll finish up together."

Luke did as asked, then helped his wife pack the remaining CSA boxes.

They worked in silence for several minutes.

Mary sealed a box and turned to Luke. "Your parents would be proud."

Luke's father had been a farmer, growing feed corn and soybeans. He'd died from brain cancer four years ago, likely linked to the chemicals he had used on their farm. His mother had died shortly thereafter, Luke thought from a broken heart. His parents' passing had inspired Luke to grow organic produce.

Luke shrugged. "What would they be proud of? My ability to borrow money?"

Mary stepped to her husband and grabbed his hand.

He turned from the box to his wife.

"I signed up three new people today. It's working. You just have to have faith."

CHAPTER 3: CURTIS AND GANDHI

The basement smelled faintly of mold. A dropped ceiling overhead covered various pipes and wires. A handful of ceiling tiles had water damage. Curtis sat on the brown couch with his girlfriend, Tisha. His best friend, Daryl, sat in a La-Z-Boy, facing the couch.

Curtis was tall and thin, with a baby face that made him appear younger than his actual age of twenty. "We need to protest these red-light cameras," Curtis said. "They shortened the yellow light time to get more tickets."

Curtis and Tisha had recently created Justice for Carville, a nonprofit focused on eliminating superfluous laws that disproportionately harmed the poor and people of color.

Tisha said, "More tickets bring more revenue to the police. We're paying for our own oppression. We should organize a march to the courthouse."

Curtis nodded to his girlfriend. "I agree."

"Ain't nobody gonna give a fuck about some red-light cameras," Daryl said, shaking his head. "You two'll be the only motherfuckers marchin'. Some nigga's gonna have to die for people to give a fuck."

"This is how it starts, Daryl," Tisha said, talking with her hands. "They get thousands of people running red lights. Some of those people can't afford the ticket, so they end up with a court date. If they can't pay the ticket, they sure as hell won't pay the court costs or even bother to show up."

Curtis watched his girlfriend, enthralled by her passion. Her braided hair hung to her chin. Her gold hoop earrings matched her nose ring. Around Carville, she was known as the black J. Lo, mostly for her figure.

Tisha continued. "Then there's a warrant out for them. Before they know it, they're in prison for being poor. They lose their license and their job, and then what are they supposed to do? Everybody wants these people to get a job, but how are they supposed to get a job with a record and no license?"

"The system is predatory," Curtis said. "It perpetuates this cycle of disproportionately criminalizing poor black and brown people."

"It's white supremacy, doing what white supremacy does." Tisha snapped her tongue off the roof of her mouth. "I'm sick of this shit. We need to do something about it."

Daryl rocked back in the La-Z-Boy. "It still won't matter. We need some dramatic shit to go down in Carville, like George Floyd or Tamir Rice or Philando Castile."

Curtis frowned at his friend.

"That's facts." Daryl stood from the La-Z-Boy and stretched his long limbs, his hands easily touching the dropped ceiling. He pointed to Curtis and Tisha on the couch. "You two can miss me with this marchin'. It won't do shit but wear out my Jordans."

Tisha stood from the couch. "Gandhi said, 'Whatever you do will be insignificant, but it is very important that you do it.'"

"Gandhi?" Daryl chuckled. "That motherfucker was racist." Daryl raised his hood over his head. "Wake me up when you got somethin' big." Then he left.

Tisha turned to Curtis, her brow furrowed. "Was Gandhi racist?"

Chapter 4: Lizzie and Quotas

Lizzie woke to the smell of coffee. Her eyes fluttered. Sunlight filtered between the blinds. She checked the clock on her bedside table and shot upright, her heart pounding. *Shit.*

Lizzie ran from her bedroom in her pajamas, down the hall, to the kitchen. Brad handed lunches to their children, wearing his police uniform.

He kissed six-year-old Emma on the head and said, "Have a good day, sweetheart." Then he mussed eight-year-old Brian's hair and said, "Be a good boy. Watch out for your sister."

"Okay, Dad," Brian replied.

Emma pointed at Lizzie and giggled. "Look at Mommy's hair."

Lizzie felt her blond hair. One side was smushed to her face, and the other side was frizzy.

Brad turned around, winked at Lizzie, then went back to the children. "Get goin', you two. You're gonna miss the bus."

"Have a good day. I love you," Lizzie called out.

But the kids were already out the door.

Lizzie met Brad near the kitchen table. Breakfast plates held the remnants of maple syrup. She ran her hands through her hair, trying to fix her bedhead, knowing that Brad preferred her to be well-kept. "I'm so sorry. I don't think my alarm went off."

Brad shook his head.

Lizzie stiffened, bracing herself.

"I turned it off. I thought you could use some extra sleep. I made you some coffee too."

She exhaled, her body relaxing. "Oh, … thank you."

"Look. I'm sorry about last night. I'm … stressed. These fuckin' quotas. I'm behind, and today's the last day of the week for me, which means I'll have to be a dick today. I *hate* bustin' people for ticky-tacky bullshit."

"They're breaking the law. That's not your fault."

Brad sat at the kitchen table, his shoulders slumped. "It's not that simple."

Lizzie sat next to him, concern etched on her face.

Brad continued. "Everyone's breakin' the laws. I choose what laws to enforce and *who* to bust. I'm not bustin' rich people from Arbor Heights. Like everyone else, I go for the low-hangin' fruit. The rowhouses in Carville. The trailer parks in Mountain View."

Lizzie tilted her head. "I don't understand."

"If I pull over some dude with shiny rims and thumpin' rap comin' from his speakers, chances are I'll find some shit. Expired registration. Window tint that's too dark. Drugs maybe. Outstandin' warrant even. I can sometimes get four or five tickets on one traffic stop. If I pull over a guy from Arbor Heights, he might know a judge or a district attorney. No doubt he can afford a good lawyer."

"I didn't know that."

Brad shrugged. "Nobody ever wants to see me, that's for sure. All day, every day, I spend my time ruinin' people's days. Sometimes their lives." Brad ran his hand over his face and hung his head.

Lizzie reached out and covered his hand with hers. "I didn't know you felt like this."

Brad met Lizzie's gaze. "I've been thinkin' about quittin'. A buddy of mine from the army sent me an email a few weeks ago. He has a private security business in Philly."

"He offered you a job?"

"Yeah. The pay is less than what I'm makin' now. The benefits aren't as good either, but I wouldn't have to deal with all this bullshit."

Lizzie retracted her hand. "But ... what about the house? The kids' college fund? Health care?"

Brad stood from the table. "Yeah, I know. We can't afford it."

Lizzie stood. "I'm just saying we have obligations."

He snatched his keys from the counter and scowled at Lizzie. "Don't worry. I'll suck it up."

Lizzie held out her hands. "That's not what I'm saying."

Brad left the house, slamming the door on his way out.

CHAPTER 5: LUKE AND MITES

Luke walked among the outdoor rows, checking the red radishes, turnips, beets, and lettuce. Morning dew still coated the plants. Sun warmed the soil. The red tops of the radish bulbs were visible and ready to pick. The golden beets needed another week. He stopped along his lettuce crop and kneeled, checking the base of a plant, and the underside of a leaf.

Tiny white mites sucked precious juice along the veins of the lettuce leaf. He checked the surrounding lettuce plants. He found a few more mites, but the outbreak was still very young and treatable. He went to his shed near the greenhouse and grabbed a plastic container labeled neem oil, which was an organic insecticide. From the lightness, Luke knew it was nearly empty.

He walked back to his farmhouse and stuck his head into the kitchen, his dirty boots still planted on the stoop. Mary did the dishes from breakfast, while Abby rocked back and forth in her swinging chair.

"I'm going to Mason's. I'll be right back," Luke said, referring to Mason's Farm & Feed.

Mary turned from the dishes. "Okay. Love you."

"Love you too."

CHAPTER 6: CURTIS MEETS CAPTAIN CRUNCH

Curtis sat at the kitchen table, eating Cap'n Crunch.

Chatter came from his police scanner. "We have a ten-ninety-one *L* at Oak Mill Park."

"Ten-four. I'll be there in five minutes."

A 10-91L was a leash law violation. *They got nothing better to do than fuck with people and their dogs.*

His phone buzzed with a text.

Daryl: Can't make it. Busy

Curtis frowned at his phone, then thumb-typed a reply.

Curtis: Busy? Doing what?

Daryl: Don't worry about it

Curtis set down his phone unnecessarily hard. *Shit.* He had asked Daryl to film him for his YouTube channel, Carville Cop Watch. It was easier to interact with the police with a cameraman. Daryl had agreed, but it wasn't unlike him to flake out.

Curtis went to the sink, rinsed his bowl, and put it in the dishwasher. Curtis's father, Leonard, walked into the kitchen with heavy boots. He was a compact man, who was in good shape for his age.

"Mornin'," Leonard said.

Curtis lifted his chin, then grabbed his phone and police scanner from the table. "See you later."

Leonard held up his hand. "Hold on. Where you goin'?"

"I'm riding downtown for content."

Leonard let out a breath. "I don't like you messin' with them cops. You're pokin' a hornet's nest. You're bound to get stung."

Curtis held up his phone. "That's what the video's for."

Leonard rubbed his beard that was more gray than black. "Look. I could really use some help today. The rain on Monday and Tuesday put me behind. I'll pay time and a half."

Leonard owned a landscaping company that serviced Carville and the surrounding suburbs. His business was a one-man band, occasionally getting help from Curtis when he was desperate.

"I can't, Dad."

Leonard frowned. "Ain't nobody stoppin' you."

Curtis shoved his phone in the front pocket of his jeans. "Maybe next week."

"How much you makin' on this YouTube thing?"

"It's growing."

"You didn't answer my question."

Curtis exhaled. "Not much yet."

"At some point you're gonna want a house of your own. A family. You need money for that."

Curtis clipped the police scanner to his belt and covered it with his hoodie. "I gotta go." He left the kitchen via the side door.

"Call me if you get done early," Leonard said to Curtis's back.

Curtis stepped into the morning sun. He unlocked his mountain bike, chained to the porch. Leonard's Chevy 2500 pickup was parked in the driveway, with an attached trailer. The sign on the truck door read Leonard & Sons Landscaping. The *sons* addition was more wishful thinking than reality.

It was a short ride to the Carville city limits. Along the way, Curtis pedaled past strip malls, fast-food restaurants, and gas stations. His police scanner mentioned a 10-38, otherwise known as a traffic stop, very close to Curtis's location.

Police lights flashed in the distance, causing Curtis to pedal faster.

A police car was parked in the feedstore parking lot to the right of the building, behind a dented Toyota Corolla with tinted windows, chrome wheels, and an exhaust the diameter of a coffee can. A bald, muscular officer strutted to the driver's side window of the Toyota. Curtis parked his bike next to a dusty pickup, with Archer Farms lettered on the doors. He removed his phone from his pocket and started recording. He walked toward the scene, trying to hold his phone steady. Curtis stopped about twenty feet from the Toyota.

The officer handed the young Latino three tickets. "This is for the tint. This one's for the illegal exhaust. And this one's for your emissions. If you wanna avoid court, I suggest you mail the tickets to the courthouse with your payment. Address is on the back."

The young man looked like he might cry. "How much is it?"

"The amounts are on the bottom."

The Latino flipped through the tickets, his eyes bulging. "It's over $500. I can't afford this."

"Maybe you shouldn't have a car," the officer said, without emotion.

"I have to work."

The officer pivoted and walked toward his cruiser.

Curtis moved closer, his camera phone still filming.

The Latino in the Toyota drove away.

The officer mean-mugged Curtis.

Curtis checked his name tag. "Why did you pull him over, Officer Lambert?"

Officer Lambert held up his hand, like a stop sign. "Get that camera out of my face."

"I have every right to film the police."

Officer Lambert climbed into his cruiser, the driver's side window down.

Curtis stepped closer, aiming his camera phone at the open window. "How does it feel to steal $500 from the working man? You're like the reverse Robin Hood. Stealing from the poor to give to the rich."

The officer chuckled. "You think I'm rich?"

"You have more than that guy."

The officer shook his head, a smirk on his face. "Have a nice day, *sir*."

As the officer powered up his window, Curtis said, "Fucking pig."

Officer Lambert opened his door and stalked to Curtis, close enough to smell the coffee on his breath. "What the fuck did you say?"

Curtis didn't move. "You heard me." He enunciated perfectly. "Fucking. Pig."

Officer Lambert narrowed his eyes. "I could arrest you for interferin' with my traffic stop."

Curtis laughed. "You can't do shit. It's all on video."

"You're not worth it." The cop turned around.

"You're a coward."

The cop whipped back around to Curtis, his face beet red. "What the hell's your problem?"

"You and your department bullying working class people. You're all fucking cowards."

The cop touched his baton. "You think I'm a coward? I've been to Iraq, you fuckin' jagoff."

Curtis smirked at the officer. "Is that where you learned how to bully brown people?"

Officer Lambert smacked the camera phone out of Curtis's grasp, knocking it to the macadam. Curtis bent to grab it, but the officer smashed it with the heel of his boot.

Curtis stood upright and said, "What the fuck? You can't do that."

The officer's lower jaw jutted forward. "I just did."

"You'll pay for it. I'll make you an internet star." Curtis turned his head and spat on the ground.

Lambert smiled. "Turn around. Put your hands behind your back. You're under arrest for spittin' on a police officer."

Curtis drew his eyebrows together. "Fuck you. I didn't spit on you."

Officer Lambert grabbed Curtis and turned him around, wrenching his arm behind his back, sending a shooting pain through his shoulder.

Curtis struggled against the pressure. "*Ow*, my shoulder."

"Stop resistin'," Lambert said through gritted teeth.

"I'm not resisting," Curtis replied, still struggling against the officer's painful hold.

Officer Lambert swept Curtis's legs, taking him to the ground, face-first on the macadam. Curtis braced his fall with his free hand, but his knees took most of the impact. The officer was on Curtis's back now, still wrenching Curtis's arm behind his back, his shoulder feeling like it might be dislocated.

"Get the fuck off me!" Curtis kicked his legs and pushed up with his one arm, trying to buck the officer off his back.

Officer Lambert grabbed his baton and flicked his wrist, extending the metal bat. Lambert hit Curtis across the back with his baton. Curtis cried out in pain, trying to contort his body away from the baton. Lambert hit him over and over again. The last blow Curtis remembered connected with the back of his head, knocking him unconscious.

CHAPTER 7: LUKE AND THE END OF EVERYTHING

Luke set a jug of neem oil on the counter.

"Find everything you need?" Fred Mason asked, standing at the cash register. His white hair and beard were unkempt.

"I did. Thanks, Mr. Mason."

"How's the farm comin'?"

"Good, except for the mites on my lettuce."

Mr. Mason tapped the jug of neem oil. "This'll work. Be careful though. It can burn. I think the label says not to spray when it's over eighty. Or maybe it's eighty-five." He scratched his head. "I can't remember."

Luke nodded, already aware of the instructions on the label. "I'll be careful."

"How's the farm comin'?"

Luke paused for a moment, unsure if Mr. Mason was aware that he'd just asked that question. "Farm's great. Thanks for asking."

Mr. Mason tapped on the cash register. "That'll be $88.45."

Luke handed the old man a one-hundred-dollar bill.

Mr. Mason processed the transaction and handed Luke his change.

Luke shoved his cash into the front pocket of his jeans, then tilted his head, and asked, "You hear that?"

Fred Mason furrowed his wrinkled brow, listening for an instant. "Nope." Then he tapped his hearing aid. "I wouldn't trust these old artillery ears though."

"I thought I heard someone yell."

Mr. Mason handed Luke his receipt. "Maybe so."

Luke grabbed the jug of neem oil. "See you later, Mr. Mason."

"Enjoy the day. Supposed to be nice."

Luke smiled at Mr. Mason and left the store. He walked to the right side of the building, where he'd parked. When Luke turned the corner, he stopped and watched the scene, his eyes wide open. A police officer struggled to subdue a man. The officer hit the man with his baton several times across the back, then once to the head. The headshot appeared to knock the man unconscious. The man was no longer struggling, but the officer still hit him with his baton, landing shots to his upper back and shoulders.

"Hey. He's not moving," Luke shouted, fast-walking toward the scene.

The officer kept hitting the man.

Luke dropped his insecticide and ran toward the altercation, crashing into the officer, knocking the cop off the man, and stopping the beating. Luke nearly fell but righted himself and shouted again, "He's not moving."

The officer scrambled to his feet, his face beet red, his neck vein throbbing. He looked up at Luke's massive frame and said, "On the fuckin' ground. *Now.*"

Luke stepped backward, showing his palms in surrender.

The officer stalked closer to Luke, pointing at the macadam with his baton. "On the *fuckin'* ground."

Luke still backpedaled, afraid of being beaten like the unconscious man.

The officer hit Luke on the side of his leg with the baton, causing Luke to go down to one knee, pain radiating from the blow. The officer tried to hit Luke over the head, but Luke reached up, blocking the onslaught with his forearms.

Searing pain came from each blow to Luke's forearms. Adrenaline surged through Luke's body. He rose to his feet and grabbed the officer's right arm with his massive hand, stopping the blows. With his other hand, he snatched the baton from the cop's grasp.

Luke let go of the officer. The cop reached for his gun, pulling the Glock from his holster. Before the officer could aim the weapon, Luke wound up and smashed the officer with the baton, connecting with the side of the officer's bald head.

The officer fell awkwardly, face-first, like he had no motor function. His head bounced off the macadam.

Luke stared at the baton in his hand, the end covered in blood. *Dear, God. What have I done?*

Chapter 8: Curtis and the Aftermath

Curtis lay on his stomach, blinking, the world spinning around him. Emergency vehicle lights whirred overhead, in addition to the flashing lights from two police cars. The back of his head throbbed, and his upper back ached. His vision came into focus. A gigantic man lay face first on the macadam. *What the hell? Who's that guy?* The big man didn't struggle as one officer cuffed his hands behind his back, while another officer aimed his Glock at the man.

Curtis turned his head.

Two EMTs attended to Officer Lambert. A pool of blood stained the macadam around the officer's head. Another police car arrived on the scene, its siren chirping. Curtis scanned the immediate area, searching for his phone. It was six feet away and smashed, but he thought he could salvage the SIM card—and more important the video data. Curtis pushed off the ground, rising to his knees, the pain from his back and shoulders nearly taking his breath away.

Two police officers rushed toward him, their handguns drawn. Curtis instinctively raised his hands.

"Don't move," an officer said.

One officer continued to aim his handgun at Curtis, as the other cuffed Curtis's hands behind his back.

Curtis grunted as the officer tightened the handcuffs.

"On your feet," the officer said, yanking Curtis upright. Then the officer patted down Curtis, checking for weapons.

"I need to go to the hospital," Curtis said, still feeling woozy.

The officer finished the pat down and asked, "You hurt?"

Curtis nodded. "Officer Lambert hit my back and head with his baton."

The officer glared at Curtis and said, "You look fine to me."

The other officer holstered his weapon and helped escort Curtis to a police car.

Curtis surveyed the scene, as he was prodded toward the cruiser. An EMT slammed the back door to the ambulance, then hurried to the driver's seat. The siren wailed, and the lights whirred, as the ambulance drove away. Curtis wondered what happened to Officer Lambert. *Why was blood coming from his head? I didn't hit him. Did I?*

The two officers pushed Curtis into the back of a police car. Curtis hit the top of his head on the door frame on the first try. He winced from the impact, the fresh wave of pain like a hammer to his skull.

"Watch your head," an officer said.

On the second try, an officer pushed down on Curtis's head, forcing him into the back seat, and slamming the door behind him. Curtis sat upright, alone in the police car, his hands cuffed behind his back. The gigantic man sat in the back of a nearby police car, his head nearly touching the ceiling. *Who the hell is he?*

Two more police cars arrived on the scene. Curtis stared at the blood spot left by Officer Lambert. *What if he dies?*

CHAPTER 9: LIZZIE AND THE NEWS

Lizzie jammed athletic socks into Brad's drawer.

The doorbell chimed.

She left her bedroom and the laundry basket, walking down the hall, then through the living room to the front door.

The doorbell chimed again.

She glanced out the sidelight window. Julie and Dennis stood on the front stoop, which was odd because it was the middle of the workday. Dennis wore his uniform, his hat in hand. Julie was dressed in a skirt suit. Their sullen expressions matched their outfits, which was in complete contrast to their jovial demeanors at dinner the night before.

Lizzie's stomach was in knots. She opened the front door and forced a smile. "Hey, you two. What are you guys doing here?"

Dennis cleared his throat, his eyes downcast. "Can we come in?"

Lizzie stepped aside. "Of course. Is everything okay?"

Dennis and Julie entered the foyer, standing before Lizzie.

Dennis rotated his hat in his hand. "Uh, … Brad was involved in an altercation this morning."

Lizzie wrung her hands; her voice trembled. "Is he okay?"

Dennis swallowed hard. "I'm sorry, Lizzie. He's gone."

Lizzie felt weak in the knees. Her voice went up an octave. "What?"

Julie hugged Lizzie and rubbed her back. "I'm so sorry, Lizzie."

Lizzie went limp in Julie's arms, like a gelatinous blob. Julie didn't have the strength to hold her upright, so she guided her to the foyer floor, still holding her.

Like an infant, Lizzie started to cry, before she made a sound. Then the wail came, loud and clear.

CHAPTER 10: LUKE'S SIN

Luke's bound hands shook as he brought the cup of water to his lips, took a sip, and set the plastic cup back on the metal table. Detective Armstrong sat across from Luke, his hands folded on the table, a notepad and pen before him. The detective was a clean-cut big man, although not quite as large as Luke. The detective's strong jaw, birdlike nose, and squinty eyes exuded strength and suspicion.

The small square room had a two-way mirror on the north wall, and video cameras tilted down from the corners of the ceiling.

"I've sinned against God." Luke swallowed the lump in his throat. "Blessed are the peacemakers, for they will be called children of God." His eyes filled with tears. "I am no longer a child of God."

"How did you sin?" Detective Armstrong asked.

"I have forsaken my eternal bond with God by taking the life of another."

Detective Armstrong removed his phone from his suit jacket. He tapped on the screen for a minute, while Luke stared at the tabletop, tears slipping down his cheeks.

The detective read from his phone. "If we confess our sins, He is faithful and righteous to forgive us our sins and to cleanse us from all unrighteousness. John 1:9." The detective slipped his phone back in his pocket. "It's time to do the right thing, Luke. Confess your sins. Tell me what happened."

Luke sniffed back mucus and wiped his face with the sleeve of his sweatshirt. He didn't say anything for a minute.

The detective waited patiently.

Finally, Luke said, "I went to Mason's to buy some neem oil."

The detective nodded. "Go on."

"When I came out to the parking lot, I saw a police officer hitting a man with his stick."

"Was the man resisting arrest?"

"It looked like he was struggling to get the officer off his back."

The detective made a note on his notepad. "What happened next?"

"Then the man stopped struggling, but the officer kept hitting him, so I yelled at him."

"What did you say?"

"I think I said something like, *He's not moving.*"

The detective nodded again. "What happened next?"

"I ran to the officer to stop him. I knocked him off the guy. Then the officer got up and started hitting me with the stick, so I took it from him."

The detective raised his eyebrows. "What did you take from Officer Lambert?"

"I took the stick." Luke swallowed again, still trying to get rid of the lump.

The detective made another note. "Go on, Luke."

Luke's lip quivered. "The officer drew his gun, so I hit him. I thought he was going to shoot me. I didn't mean to kill him."

"Of course you didn't." The detective paused for a moment. "Why did you hit Officer Lambert with the baton?"

"He was reaching for his gun. It all happened so fast. I was scared."

Detective Armstrong tilted his head. "Are you sure he drew his weapon? The bodycam footage doesn't show that."

"I, … I don't know. I thought he was reaching for his gun."

"Police officers can and do draw their weapons to stop an attack. Do you think Officer Lambert just wanted you to drop the baton?"

"I don't know. I was afraid he'd kill me, like the man he was beating."

"That man's alive and well. His name's Curtis Mays."

Luke nodded, his gaze downcast.

"At the time you hit Officer Lambert with the baton, did you believe Curtis Mays was in fact dead?

"I didn't know."

"Did you know that Curtis routinely agitates police officers and interferes with traffic stops and routine investigations?"

Luke shook his head.

"He runs a YouTube channel called Carville Cop Watch. Let me read you some of the comments on his channel." Detective Armstrong flipped his notepad, revealing another page with his handwritten notes. *"All cops are bastards. Fuck the police. Pigs in a blanket, fry 'em like bacon. When is it okay to kill a cop? Anytime, anywhere. Cops should fear us, not the other way around."*

Luke closed his eyes.

"Look at me, Luke."

Luke opened his eyes.

"Do you have children, Luke?"

"I have a four-month-old daughter."

"You married?"

Luke nodded again.

"Officer Lambert was married too. He had two children. Brian's eight and little Emma's six. They'll never see their father again."

Tears filled Luke's eyes. "I'm sorry."

"It's time to repent, to tell the truth. I believe, if you would've put down that baton, Officer Lambert would still be alive, and you'd be at home with your wife and baby right now." Detective Armstrong leaned forward. "I need you to repent right now, Luke. If you're ever to be right with God, I need you to tell the truth. Do you really believe Officer Lambert would've killed you if you would've dropped that baton? A decorated officer who has never shot anyone?"

"It was a mistake. I'm so sorry."

Detective Armstrong was stern now. "You didn't answer my question. Do you believe Officer Lambert would've killed you if you didn't hit him in the head and kill him first?"

Luke shook his head and said, "No." Then he dissolved into tears.

CHAPTER 11: CURTIS AND THE INTERROGATION

Curtis sat at a metal desk, across from the detective, his back and head aching. "I need to go to the hospital. You can't keep me here."

Detective Armstrong shook his head. "You're not going anywhere. You're under arrest for resisting and obstruction."

"This is bullshit. I'm suing for police brutality. I have it all on video." Curtis knew this was an empty threat, as the police likely had his phone, and it was smashed to smithereens.

The detective sighed, as if he'd heard it all before. "That's your right. I've seen stronger cases get *nothing*."

Curtis clenched his jaw. "We'll see."

"If I were you, I'd be concerned about the fact that Officer Lambert's dead."

Curtis recoiled, wondering if he was somehow legally responsible for the officer's death. "He died?"

Detective Armstrong nodded. "He did. Left a wife and two young kids too. Not that you give a shit."

"I didn't have anything to do with that. All I remember is Lambert damn near beat me to death with his baton."

"Yet, you're alive, and Officer Lambert's dead."

"Like I said, I didn't have anything to do with that. Maybe that guy you all arrested had something to do with it?"

"Luke Archer?"

"I don't know his name. Some big corn-fed white boy."

The detective stared at Curtis for a few seconds. "Did you see Mr. Archer attack Officer Lambert?"

"I didn't see anything." Curtis glared at the detective. "I was unconscious."

"It's too bad you didn't see anything. You might be able to help yourself. You sure you didn't see something?"

Curtis shook his head, a scowl on his face. Curtis figured the detective wanted to hear something to strengthen their murder investigation. "This Archer guy saved my life, didn't he?"

The detective hesitated. "I, ... I highly doubt that, but we're still investigating."

Curtis let out a heavy breath. "And you expect me to make up some bullshit about the man?"

"I expect you to tell the truth."

"You're a liar. I want a lawyer."

Chapter 12: Lizzie and the Masked Man

Lizzie lay in bed, on her side, in the fetal position. The covers were pulled over her head, her eyes sealed shut. She imagined a masked man, hitting Brad over the head with a metal pipe. Brad fell to the macadam, blood spilling from his head. The masked man came into her house, crept through the kitchen, down the hall to her bedroom door. Her bedroom doorknob turned, and the masked man stepped to her bed.

He yanked the covers from Lizzie's body. She turned over on her back, holding up her hands in surrender. The masked man smashed the side of her skull with his metal pipe. She was dazed, the room spinning. He straddled her and raised the pipe. She groped for his mask, pain radiating from her skull. The man lowered the pipe and removed his mask. It was her husband.

Brad smiled, reared back, and swung the pipe, connecting with her temple.

The side door opened in the distance, jolting Lizzie from her daydream. Brian and Emma entered the house, arguing about who gets to watch the big TV. The kids always walked home from the bus stop, and Brian wore a house key around his neck. Brad thought they should learn responsibility and independence.

Lizzie climbed out of bed and met her children in the living room.

Brian stared at her, his head cocked.

Emma must've noticed Lizzie's blotchy face and asked, "What's wrong, Mommy?"

Lizzie sat on the couch and gestured to her children. "Come sit with Mommy."

Brian and Emma sat on either side of Lizzie.

Lizzie reached out and pulled her children toward her, hugging them tight. Tears welled in her eyes.

Brian wriggled from her grasp, but Emma climbed into her lap. Brian narrowed his eyes at Lizzie. "Why are you crying?"

Lizzie sniffled and wiped the corners of her eyes with the side of her index finger. "There's something I have to tell you two." Lizzie took a deep breath. "Your father." Her voice caught. "Your father." She took another deep breath. "Your father died today."

Emma gaped at her mother.

Brian's face contorted, then turned red. He wagged his head back and forth, like he was trying to shake something loose in his brain.

Tears slipped down Lizzie's cheeks. She pulled her children tight to her body. "I'm so sorry." Lizzie rubbed Brian's back, as he sobbed.

Then Emma cried for her brother more than her father. Her father's death wasn't real yet.

CHAPTER 13: LUKE AND MURDER

Luke had waited in the interview room alone for several hours, replaying his altercation with Officer Lambert in his mind. Detective Armstrong had checked on Luke periodically, asking him if he needed anything, thanking him for his patience. Despite Luke's earlier admission of guilt, he distinctly remembered Officer Lambert drawing his weapon. The ferocious beating Officer Lambert had given Luke and especially Curtis Mays made him believe that Lambert would've shot Luke, if given the chance. The more he thought about it, the more he thought he'd be dead if he hadn't hit Officer Lambert. Luke hoped that the bodycam footage would show that, and he'd be let go.

Detective Armstrong entered the interview room again. This time he carried a tablet.

Luke perked up, meeting the detective's gaze.

Armstrong frowned at Luke. "We analyzed the bodycam footage."

"What did it show?" Luke asked, still cuffed to the table.

"See for yourself." Detective Armstrong set the tablet in front of Luke and pressed Play.

The video showed Officer Lambert hit Luke on the side of his leg with the baton, causing Luke to go down to one knee. The officer tried to hit Luke over the head, but Luke blocked the onslaught with his forearms.

Luke blanched at the violence.

Detective Armstrong hovered, watching Luke's reactions to the bodycam footage.

Luke on the screen rose to his feet and grabbed the officer's right arm with his massive hand, stopping the blows. With his other hand, he snatched the baton from the cop's grasp. Luke let go of the officer. It was here that Luke remembered the cop drawing his gun from his holster, but the bodycam footage only showed what was happening in front of the officer, not what was happening at his hip. One thing was for sure, Officer Lambert didn't aim his handgun at Luke, otherwise it would've shown up on the bodycam footage.

Detective Armstrong slowed the video for the coup de grâce. Here, Luke reared back, his face red and contorted, the unfamiliar mask of fury. Then Luke swung the baton, connecting with the officer's temple, accompanied by an audible *crack*. Officer Lambert fell face-first. The video went black, the camera lens on the macadam.

Luke swallowed the bile creeping up his throat.

Detective Armstrong took the tablet and tapped on the screen, stopping the video. "There's no evidence that Officer Lambert drew his weapon."

"I thought I saw him grab his gun. He would've shot me. I'm sure of it."

The detective leaned back in his chair. "That's not what you said earlier. You said before that you weren't sure if Officer Lambert was reaching for his gun."

Luke pictured Lambert reaching for his gun. "I'm sure now."

"Then why was Officer Lambert's weapon still in his holster when we found him?"

Luke shook his head, his stomach sick. "That can't be. I don't understand. What does this mean?"

"It means you'll be charged with first-degree murder of a law enforcement officer."

Luke vomited on the tabletop.

Chapter 14: Lizzie and Chief Rhodes

The television glowed in the darkness of Lizzie's living room, the volume barely audible. The local news showed a picture of Brad in his dress blues, smiling for the camera. Lizzie lay on the couch in a trance, watching the breaking news report.

The anchorman said, "Officer Brad Lambert, a thirteen-year veteran of the Carville Police Department, was killed during a traffic stop in the parking lot of Mason's Farm & Feed in Carville. Two suspects have been apprehended."

A knock came from her side door, jolting her from her stupor. She didn't move, wondering if it had been her imagination. The knock came again. Lizzie rose from the couch, left her living room for the kitchen and the side door. She parted the curtain on the door window. Chief Dennis Rhodes stood there, his hat in hand.

Lizzie fixed her hair with her hands and looked down at her pajamas. Light blue pajama pants and a shirt, covered in little sheep. She adjusted the button-down shirt, trying to make her braless state less noticeable. Then she opened the door. "Hi, Dennis."

Dennis forced a smile, his eyes bloodshot. "Hey, Lizzie."

She stepped aside. "You want to come in?"

Dennis nodded.

They stood in the kitchen. Lizzie hugged herself, feeling self-conscious in the bright fluorescence of the kitchen.

"I'm sorry to bother you," Dennis said.

"You're no bother," Lizzie replied. "Can I get you something to drink?"

Dennis flashed his palms. "No. Thank you. I just stopped by to check on you."

"That's sweet of you. Thank you, Dennis."

"Of course."

"I'm not sure how I'm supposed to feel. I feel numb, like this is all a bad dream."

"You need time."

Lizzie sighed. "Maybe."

"How are Brian and Emma?"

"Brian cried himself to sleep. I think Emma's still processing."

"I'm sorry, Lizzie."

Lizzie swallowed hard.

"If you need help with the kids, Julie wants to help."

"My mother's coming tomorrow."

"That's good. It's good to have family around at a time like this."

Lizzie shrugged. "We'll see. My mother isn't the easiest woman to live with."

Dennis cleared his throat. "Well, I should get—"

"Who is he? The man who killed my husband."

Dennis hesitated, then said, "Luke Archer. He's a local farmer."

Lizzie shook her head. "Why? Why did he do it?"

"Claims Brad was gonna kill him."

Lizzie's legs wobbled.

Dennis stepped forward and put his arm around Lizzie's waist to steady her. "You okay?"

"I should sit."

Dennis led her to a chair at the kitchen table, where Lizzie sat down. "Have you had anything to eat today?"

Lizzie shook her head again. "I haven't been hungry."

"You need to eat. Can I make you something?"

"No. I'm fine."

Dennis stood over her, with arched eyebrows. "Really?"

"Yes. *Really.*"

Dennis gaped at her for a long beat.

Lizzie adjusted her shirt, feeling self-conscious again.

"Well, I should get outta your hair," Dennis said, reaching into his breast pocket and removing a pen and business card. "Do you have my cell number?"

"I don't think so."

Dennis wrote the number on the back of his card and handed it to Lizzie. "If you need anything, and I mean *anything*, you call me. Anytime, day or night."

Lizzie took the card and gazed into Dennis's eyes. "I need Luke Archer to go to prison *forever*."

CHAPTER 15: LUKE'S ARRAIGNMENT

After the weekend at the Carville Jail, Luke sat in a holding cell in the basement of the Carville Courthouse. His hands and feet were cuffed, and he wore an orange jumpsuit. Two sheriff's deputies opened his cell and escorted him to an elevator. Luke shuffled from the leg cuffs. They took the elevator to the third floor. The deputies escorted Luke down a back hallway and through a door labeled Courtroom 3C.

The courtroom was packed, the audience sitting on rows of wooden pews. Many uniformed Carville police officers were in attendance, each with a strip of black tape across their badges. The pews were separated by a short wooden divider from everything else—the tables for the prosecution and the defense, the tall desk for the judge and witnesses, and a jury box with twelve empty chairs.

Luke scanned the audience, as he was escorted to the defense table, spotting Mary in the second row. Her eyes were red-rimmed, but she gave him a small smile. Luke returned a discreet wave. He sat next to the public defender, who he had met an hour ago. The judge presided over them from his tall desk.

Luke had had so many questions, but the public defender only had ten minutes to spare. She spoke a mile a minute, Luke only retaining the most important part. *Not guilty.* The public defender, Gina Walters, assumed he would plead not guilty, but Luke was on the fence, knowing he had sinned and deserved to be punished.

A name placard in front of the judge read Honorable Harry Malone. A crescent of white hair ringed his bald head. His face had deep grooves, more than wrinkles, and bags under his eyes, as if his career of judgments had aged him severely. Reading from a file, he said, "This is case number twenty-one-dash-three-seven-eight-two, the Commonwealth of Pennsylvania versus Luke Archer. The defendant has been charged with the first-degree murder of a law enforcement officer, a violation of Title 25 of the Pennsylvania Code, Section 2507, subsection A, which carries a maximum sentence of death and a minimum mandatory sentence of life in prison."

A few people in the audience gasped.

Luke dropped his gaze. Gina Walters sat ramrod straight next to him, looking up to the judge, her dark hair in a tight bun.

Judge Malone raised his gaze from the file. "In the matter of the Commonwealth of Pennsylvania versus Luke Archer, how do you plead?"

Gina nodded to Luke.

Luke looked up, opened his mouth, but nothing came out.

Judge Malone scowled. "Mr. Archer. How do you plead?"

"I don't know," Luke said, barely above a whisper.

"Speak up, Mr. Archer."

"I don't know."

"May I have a couple of minutes with my client, Your Honor?" Gina asked.

The judge glared at Gina. "Be quick, Counselor. We do not have all day."

Gina turned to Luke and spoke to him in a hushed whisper. "I thought we talked about this? All you have to say is *not guilty*."

Luke wrung his hands, his head bowed. He whispered back, "I sinned against God. I'm guilty of taking a life."

"I know we just met, but the right thing to do is to plead *not* guilty. If you really want to change your plea later and make a deal, you can. It's rare that the commonwealth won't offer you a plea deal. ... Do you mind if I give you a little advice?"

Luke nodded, noticing the crucifix pendant hanging from her necklace.

Gina leaned in, still talking in a hushed whisper. "This court isn't here to act as your God's proxy. This court will judge you according to the laws of man. Your God will judge you in the afterlife. If your God disagrees, this is not the venue for His punishment."

Luke swallowed hard, thinking about Mary and Abby. He took a deep breath. "Okay. I'll plead not guilty."

Judge Malone asked Luke for his plea again.

This time Luke said, "Not guilty."

Judge Malone leafed through his planner. "I'd like to set the pre-liminary hearing for ten days from today, Thursday, May 20 at 8:30 a.m. Ms. Walters?"

"That'll be fine, Your Honor."

Judge Malone addressed the dark-haired man, sitting behind the prosecutor's table. "Mr. Perkins?"

"That works for the commonwealth, Your Honor," District Attorney Perkins replied.

Judge Malone made a note in his planner, then addressed the prosecuting attorney again. "I'll hear from the commonwealth regarding bail."

DA Perkins rose from his seat. He was tall, dark, and likely used to be handsome, until middle age had carved lines in his face, and first-world abundance had built a paunch under his three-piece suit. "Given that a law enforcement officer was murdered in the line of duty, and the minimum mandatory sentence is life in prison, we believe Mr. Archer is a serious flight risk and a danger to the community."

Judge Malone eyed the prosecuting attorney. "Mr. Perkins, does the commonwealth have a recommended bail amount?"

"We're recommending bail be set at one million dollars."

Luke didn't flinch at the exorbitant amount, knowing that he and Mary didn't have $5,000 much less one million.

Judge Malone looked at Gina. "Ms. Walters?"

Gina Walters rose from her seat. "This is egregious. One million dollars is double the recommended amount of the bail schedule for this charge. Mr. Archer is not a flight risk. He does not have a criminal record."

Judge Malone frowned. "I agree with Mr. Perkins. This may be double the recommended amount for a first-degree murder charge, but we have to take into account that this is the murder of a law enforcement officer. I'll set bail at $1,000,000—with a mandatory electronic monitoring device ordered if bail is met." He banged his gavel.

CHAPTER 16: CURTIS'S ARRAIGNMENT

A name placard in front of the judge read Honorable Francine Humphrey. She was middle-aged with dark curly hair. Her black robe nearly swallowed her petite frame. She read aloud from a file, "This is case number twenty-one-dash-three-seven-nine-zero, the Commonwealth of Pennsylvania versus Curtis Mays. The defendant has been charged with one count of obstructing administration of law, a violation of Title 18 of the Pennsylvania Code, Section 5101, subsection B. This is a second-degree misdemeanor that carries a maximum sentence of two years in prison and a $5,000 fine."

Curtis sat next to the public defender, suppressing a scowl, still nursing a dull headache and a sore back. Curtis wasn't impressed with the pudgy man who'd been assigned to his case an hour ago. The public defender, Hugh Ellis, had already advised Curtis to plea bargain. The public defender had boasted that he could make a deal with the prosecution to avoid prison time. Curtis had said, "Fuck that. I didn't do anything wrong."

Judge Humphrey looked up from the file. "The defendant has also been charged with one count of resisting arrest, a violation of Title 18 of the Pennsylvania Code, Section 5104. This is a second-degree misdemeanor that carries a maximum sentence of two years in prison and a $5,000 fine." The judge sipped water from the glass on her desk, then eyed Curtis. "In the matter of the Commonwealth of Pennsylvania versus Curtis Mays, how do you plead?"

Curtis replied, "Not guilty."

Judge Humphrey checked her planner. "How's Wednesday, May 19 at 8:30 a.m. for the preliminary hearing?"

The prosecution and defense attorneys agreed to the date and time.

Judge Humphrey addressed the heavyset woman, sitting behind the prosecutor's table. "I'll hear from the commonwealth regarding bail."

"Given that the defendant's careless actions led to the death of a police officer, the commonwealth is seeking a $10,000 bail," the prosecutor replied.

Curtis glared at the prosecutor.

Judge Humphrey skimmed the file, flipping through the pages. Then she addressed the public defender. "Mr. Ellis?"

The public defender rose from his seat. "These are misdemeanor charges. ROR is appropriate here. The police officer was killed by a man unrelated and unknown to my client. In fact, my client was unconscious at the time of the alleged murder, due to the severe beating suffered from the aforementioned police officer."

Judge Humphrey nodded. "I agree with Mr. Ellis. The defendant is to be released on his own recognizance." She banged her gavel.

A quick cheer came from the audience. Curtis glanced over his shoulder at the mostly empty pews. Tisha and Daryl sat in the front row, big smiles on their faces. Curtis's father sat nearby, a scowl on his face.

CHAPTER 17: LIZZIE'S MOM

Birds chirped and walked on the metal gutters near Lizzie's bedroom window. Morning sun slipped through the curtains. Lizzie covered her head with her pillow. The birds squawked now. Probably a territorial dispute.

Lizzie threw her pillow on the floor and rolled on her back. She stared at the ceiling, hypnotized by the ceiling fan. Several minutes later, she slipped out of bed, headed for the bathroom.

As she brushed her teeth, she stared at her horrific appearance. Her face was blotchy. Her eyes and nostrils were rimmed with red. Her dark roots were noticeable. She needed a fresh dye job.

After the bathroom, she stepped down the hall, peering into Brian's and Emma's rooms. Neither child was there. She found her mother in Brad's home office, sitting at his desk, pouring over stacks of papers.

"What are you doing?" Lizzie asked. "Where are the kids?"

Helen looked up from the papers. "I'm organizing your finances. Brad left an absolute mess. And the kids are at school."

Lizzie glowered at her mother. "Why would you send them to school without asking me? They're not ready."

"They wanted to go to school." Helen looked Lizzie up and down. "Sitting around here moping won't help them or *you* for that matter."

Lizzie tensed, the criticism bringing a wave of familiar childhood guilt. Lizzie almost said, *Fuck you*, but swallowed her anger instead and gestured to the papers. "I can handle that."

Helen tilted her head, giving Lizzie an *I doubt that* look. "You can barely get out of bed."

"My husband just died!" Lizzie shouted.

It had only been three days since Brad's death.

Helen frowned. "Do you want my help or not? I'm not doing this for my health."

"Why don't you just go home? I don't need your criticisms right now."

Helen stood from the desk. "You'll have to talk to the funeral director. They need some decisions. The Carville Police Department will cover three thousand dollars, but there's paperwork. The state has funeral benefits too. Then there's Brad's police life insurance. You'll also have to decide whether you want a lump sum benefit or 66 percent of Brad's salary."

Lizzie's eyes glazed over, and her shoulders slumped.

"The kids will be eligible for free college. The mortgage needs to be paid too and the utility bills. Brad wasn't great at paying promptly. The light bill is already late. I was going to call them and ask them to waive the late fees, given the circumstances. Can you survive on 66 percent of Brad's salary?"

"What?"

Helen sighed. "Can you survive on 66 percent of Brad's salary?"

"I, uh, … I don't know."

"Thought so. I was going to prepare a financial statement for you and a budget based on the insurance benefits you're eligible for, but I'm sure *you* can figure it out." Helen walked around the desk and approached Lizzie. "I should get my stuff."

Lizzie bowed her head. "Don't go."

CHAPTER 18: LUKE AND FAITH

Separated by polycarbonate "glass," Luke told Mary exactly what had happened in the parking lot of Mason's Farm & Feed.

"I know you, Luke," Mary replied, a phone receiver to her ear. "You wouldn't hit anybody, unless you were protecting yourself or somebody else. In this case it was both."

Luke nodded, anguish on his face, also with a phone receiver pressed to his ear. "I was angry. I hit that man in anger."

"You're allowed to be angry."

Luke hung his head. "It's a sin to kill."

"Look at me."

Luke raised his gaze.

"You did what you had to do to survive, to come home to us."

"But I'm not coming home."

Tears welled in Mary's eyes.

"I'm so sorry, Mary. As God is my witness, I'll never commit another act of violence as long as I live, but I still owe a penance for what I've done."

"You don't owe *anybody.*"

Luke pressed his lips together, disagreeing, but not wanting to cause Mary more pain and anguish.

"I can't fight for you if you won't fight for us." Tears slipped down her cheeks. "Please don't give up on us, Luke. I need you to fight this."

Luke nodded again, sniffing, and fighting his own tears.

Mary removed a handkerchief from her purse and wiped her face. Then she said, "I don't know what to do. I can't run the farm and take care of Abby all by myself. We can't afford to hire a farmhand."

"I know." Luke thought about his parents, wishing they were still alive. His father would've taken over the farm chores, and his mother would've helped with Abby. "I only need you to keep the bare minimum going, until I get out of here. The planting schedule's on my desk. You'll need to harvest whatever's ripe toward the end of next week, then deliver the CSA baskets to the pickup locations on Saturday and Sunday. And the lettuce crop has mites. You need to spray it with neem oil as soon as possible."

"I can't do it without you."

"You know how to farm. You grew up farming."

Mary grew up on an Amish farm. She did far more cooking and sewing than farming, but she did know how to farm.

"Maybe you could call your parents for help?" Luke asked.

Mary stiffened and shook her head. "You know that's not possible."

"It's worth a try—"

"*No.*"

"I'm sorry. I shouldn't have suggested it."

Mary pursed her lips. "It's okay. I'll figure it out."

A guard walked behind Luke and the other inmates at the partitioned visiting room. "One minute. One minute."

"We'll have to put our faith in God," Luke said.

Mary nodded, noncommittal.

CHAPTER 19: CURTIS AND CONSEQUENCES

In the parking lot, outside the courthouse and jail, Curtis hugged Tisha. It was unseasonably warm. Then he gave Daryl a less intimate bro hug, with a pat on the back.

Curtis gasped at the pat on his back that was a little too hard, but nobody noticed his pain.

After they separated, Daryl shook his head. "I fucked up. I should've been there."

"You didn't know. Shit, I didn't know," Curtis replied. "That cop lost his fucking mind. I thought he was going to kill me."

Curtis's dad, Leonard, interrupted the trio. He pointed at Curtis. "In the truck. Let's go."

"I'll catch a ride with Tisha," Curtis replied.

Leonard clenched his jaw. "Get your ass in the truck. *Now.*"

Curtis turned to his friends. "I'll text you all later."

Tisha kissed him on the cheek and whispered into his ear, "You didn't do anything wrong."

Curtis followed his father to the Chevy 2500, his shoulders slumped in anticipation of what was to come. The door creaked as Curtis opened the passenger door and climbed into the truck.

Leonard drove away from the courthouse toward home. He didn't say a word for the first few minutes. Curtis peered out the window at the Carville city rowhouses, and the old ladies sitting on their front porches, enjoying the beautiful spring day.

"I ain't got time for this shit today," Leonard announced. "You know what it's like in the spring."

Curtis huffed. "I didn't ask you to come to court."

"Someone had to bail your ass out."

43

"I didn't need bail."

Leonard scowled at his son, then turned back to the road. "You didn't know that."

"I know the charges are bullshit."

Leonard turned the truck onto Valley Road unnecessarily fast. They drove past a gas station, a pawn shop, and several fast-food joints. Leonard stared straight ahead, gripping the steering wheel and gritting his teeth.

"I don't know why you're mad at me. I didn't do anything. Got my ass kicked for nothing."

Leonard turned into a strip mall, parking in the mostly empty lot. Half of the stores were unoccupied, with lease signs in the windows. Leonard slammed the truck into Park and glared at Curtis. "*Nothin*? You gonna tell me you did *nothin*?"

Curtis dipped his head.

"I've seen your videos, boy. Provokin' these cops. Callin' 'em cowards and pigs and worse. Gettin' in their faces. Stickin' your nose and your camera into their business."

Curtis turned to his father. "Someone has to hold these cops accountable. The fact that that crazy-ass cop went off is exactly why I do what I do. That piece of shit almost killed me."

"But here you are. Alive and well, while one man's dead, and another's prob'ly goin' to prison for life."

Curtis looked away, a lump in his throat.

"That cop was married. Two kids. The man who saved your ass? Luke Archer? I looked him up too. He's married with a newborn. You gonna take care of their kids now?" Leonard blew out a breath. "You can't even take care of yourself."

CHAPTER 20: LIZZIE AND THE EULOGY

Lizzie sat in the front row of the cavernous Catholic Church, flanked by her children and mother. Sunlight filtered through the stained glass, casting an ethereal glow. The church was packed with police officers, wearing their dress blues, and well-dressed civilians all in black. Every seat was taken, with many standing in the back, but you could hear a pin drop as Chief Dennis Rhodes walked across the platform to the podium. Flowers decorated the altar behind Dennis.

He adjusted the microphone. "Some people say law enforcement is a profession, but, for most of us who wear the badge, it's a calling. I can't think of a calling more noble than the protection of your community. But this profession comes with a heavy price." Dennis took a deep breath. "We pay with our blood, sweat, and tears, and sometimes our lives. Our families suffer too, the specter of danger always there. The bravest among us answer the call to become a police officer."

Lizzie sniffled, tears welling in her eyes. She held Brian's hand as he stared zombielike at the floor. Her other arm hugged little Emma tight to her body, who buried her head in Lizzie's chest.

Dennis continued. "Officer Bradley Lambert joined the Carville Police Department thirteen years ago. I remember his first day like it was yesterday. He responded to a serious car accident. A mother in a minivan with two kids in the back hit a telephone pole. He was the first on the scene. His job was to secure the scene until the paramedics arrived, but the minivan caught fire. Brad didn't hesitate. He carried that mother and her two children to safety, just before the minivan was engulfed in flames."

Dennis paused, letting the story linger for a moment. "Brad served this community with the highest distinction. He never hesitated to run toward danger, to provide aid and protection to those in need. He was the bravest of the brave." Dennis scanned the audience. "The turnout today is

45

a tribute to Officer Lambert's exceptional service to our community. It's a tribute to his dedication to his wife and children, to his friends, and to his fellow officers. He will be sorely missed by us all."

Tears slipped down Lizzie's cheeks. She thought about the goodness in her late-husband. The protectiveness. The strength. The loyalty. The commitment. At the same time, she couldn't shake the guilty feeling of relief that he was gone.

Dennis said, "God bless you, Brad. May you rest in peace."

CHAPTER 21: MARY AND BURDENED

Mary stepped outside, her baby monitor in the breast pocket of her overalls. The bright sun warmed her skin. She went to the shed and grabbed the jug of neem oil that Fred Mason had dropped off, along with their pickup truck. Fred hadn't made any small talk or even eye contact. He had been quick to leave in another truck. It had reminded Mary of how her Amish friends had treated her when she had left the community.

Mary read the instructions.

Mix one fluid ounce per gallon water. Do not add adjuvants to this product. *What's an adjuvant?* Shake well before using. For optimal performance, do not mix with cold water.

The crunch of gravel interrupted her. A gray sedan crept up her driveway. Mary set down the jug of neem oil and walked toward the sedan. It parked behind their pickup truck. A woman exited the vehicle, her cell phone in hand.

The woman waved and smiled as she approached, as if she knew Mary.

Mary waved back, not wanting to be rude.

The woman said, "Mary Archer?"

"Yes?" Mary replied.

The woman snapped three quick pictures with her phone. "Hi, I'm Jennifer Talbot, with the *Carville Chronicle*. I was hoping you could answer a few questions about your husband."

Mary drew her eyebrows together. "I have to get back to work."

The woman stepped closer. "Would you have time later today or tomorrow?"

Mary shook her head. "Oh, I don't know. I don't think I should talk about it."

"Don't you want people to hear your side of the story? Your husband's side? People are calling your husband a murderer and a cop killer."

"I don't want to talk to you. Please leave."

"What will you do if your husband's convicted? He's facing life in prison or possibly the death penalty."

Mary felt sick to her stomach. "Please leave. I don't want you here."

The woman handed Mary a business card, one side of her mouth raised in contempt. "If you change your mind."

Mary took the card, and the woman left. Mary went back to the neem oil, unable to concentrate on the task at hand, the woman's words reverberating in her brain. *Life in prison or possibly the death penalty. People are calling your husband a murderer. A cop killer.*

Mary mixed the neem oil in a backpack sprayer. One ounce of concentrate per gallon of water. She hefted the sprayer on her back, the thirty-five-pounds of liquid a struggle for her tiny frame. She sprayed the row of lettuce, the burden lifting as the liquid left the sprayer. She was nearly empty as she sprayed the last lettuce plants.

She returned the sprayer to the shed and removed the seed schedule from her pocket. She needed to plant cucumbers, squash, melons, and zucchini. The schedule also indicated which rows to plant. Mary peered down the long row, trying to remember if Luke had a special tool to help with the task. Mary had used a diamond hoe when she was a girl.

Crying came from her baby monitor. Mary jogged back to the house and went to Abby's room. While she breastfed her baby, Mary thought about the long hours Luke worked on the farm. She cried softly as Abby suckled her breast. *I can't do this.*

CHAPTER 22: CURTIS AND THE DEBT

Curtis and Daryl descended the basement steps. Curtis sat on the couch gingerly, his back still bruised from the beating. His four-day headache had finally subsided after ice and ibuprofen, but he still had a knot on the back of his head. "Thanks for coming."

Daryl sat on the old La-Z-Boy, facing the couch. "What's this about?"

"Let's wait for Tisha."

Curtis had texted Daryl and Tisha to meet in Curtis's basement that Tuesday at noon, but he purposely hadn't given any specifics, worried that they wouldn't show if they knew.

Tisha descended the basement steps, her leggings showing off her curves. If it was anyone else, Daryl might've said, "Damn, girl."

Curtis stood from the couch, gave his girlfriend a kiss, and they sat together.

"Your dad's pretty pissed, huh?" Tisha asked.

"Yeah. He thinks this shit is all my fault because I was in the cop's face," Curtis replied.

"No disrespect to your pops, but that ain't true," Daryl said. "If that motherfucker will beat a nigga down on video, what you think he did when nobody was watchin'?"

Tisha snapped her fingers several times. "You're right, Daryl."

"What's this secret meetin' about?" Daryl asked.

"Luke Archer," Curtis said.

"What about him?" Tisha asked.

Curtis turned in his seat toward Tisha. "You've seen how the media's painting him as a cop killer."

Tisha shrugged. "In the local media maybe, but mainstream media hasn't even covered the story."

Curtis tilted his head. "You wonder why that is? If Luke was a black man, this would be national news, but it doesn't fit their narrative."

"What *narrative?*"

"The last thing they want is a story about a white man helping a black man. They want us divided by race, class, and political party. As long as we're fighting each other, we'll never fight the power structure."

Daryl pointed at Curtis. "He's gotta point."

Tisha rolled her eyes. "Sounds like a conspiracy theory to me."

"Either way. White boy's fucked. You kill a cop, they don't even care if you're white," Daryl said.

"He has a wife and a new baby. You know that?" Curtis asked, making eye contact with Daryl, then Tisha.

"That's tough," Tisha replied, her eyes downcast. "I wish he would've just knocked that cop out."

"He ain't never gettin' out," Daryl added.

"I think we should do something to help him," Curtis said.

"Like what?" Tisha asked.

"We could stage a march and rally to the police station. Demand his release," Curtis said.

Daryl snickered. "Y'all know what I think. That ain't gonna do shit. No way in hell they let him go."

Curtis frowned at his friend. "I know that, but we need to shift the narrative. Let people know that some people think he's innocent, that it was self-defense."

"Do we know that?" Tisha asked, holding out her hands. "They got enough evidence to try the man for murder. And they got it on video. What does that tell you?"

"What if he was a black man?"

"He's not."

Curtis shook his head. "Don't do that. You and I both know you'd be saying that it was police brutality and that the man had every right to defend himself. I know you."

Tisha smacked her tongue off the roof of her mouth. "You're not in my head. You don't know what I think. If we support him, and he's convicted, Justice for Carville's finished." Justice for Carville was their newly formed nonprofit. "We're making connections. We just hooked up with BLM Philly."

"I contacted Amari. He's down. Already put it out for his people." Amari was their contact at BLM Philly.

Tisha pulled back. "You did that behind my back."

"Because I knew this is how you'd react."

Tisha rose from the couch, looking down on Curtis, her hands on her hips. "When is it?"

Curtis broke eye contact. "Tomorrow."

"*Tomorrow*? When did you contact Amari?"

"Yesterday."

"Why didn't you tell me then?"

"Because I didn't think they'd agree to march."

Daryl raised his hand. "Hold on. Do they know the man's white?"

Curtis cleared his throat. "I told them he was half-Colombian."

Daryl burst into laughter.

Tisha spoke, her neck moving back and forth. "What the hell is wrong with you, Curtis? Are you crazy? When they find out you lied, they'll never do anything with us again."

Curtis stood from the couch, showing his palms in surrender. "He has a tan in his mugshot. He can pass."

Daryl doubled over with laughter.

"Either way, he risked his life for a black man."

"You should've told the truth," Tisha said.

"They never would've agreed to help," Curtis replied. "Remember that police shooting in Minneapolis? BLM went home when they found out the victim was white."

"That's not why they went home. The guy was a carjacker, and he was shooting at the police."

Daryl stood from the La-Z-Boy, his laughter subsiding. "I'm out."

"Will you march tomorrow?" Curtis asked.

"Naw. Not my thing." Daryl started up the basement steps.

"Is it because he's white?"

Daryl stopped on the stairwell. "I don't know. I do feel some type a way about him bein' white, but marchin' ain't gonna change shit anyway." Daryl left the basement.

Tisha watched Daryl leave, then she turned back to Curtis. "I should go too."

"You're not marching either, are you?"

"You're making all the decisions without me. Why should I participate?"

"Because that man saved my life."

"You don't know that for sure," Tisha said. "You were unconscious."

Curtis moved closer to his girlfriend. "You didn't see the look in that cop's eyes. He was going to kill me. Believe that."

Tisha held out her hands. "What if he wasn't? We could've had a national news police brutality case to jumpstart our charity. Now everyone's mourning this cop."

Curtis raised one side of his mouth in disgust. "Listen to yourself. You'd rather I risk death for some fucking news cred?"

"That's not what I'm saying. I'm just saying, you don't owe this white man anything." Tisha raised her chin, pivoted, and left the basement.

"You're wrong," Curtis called out to her back. "I owe him *everything*."

Chapter 23: Luke and the Plea Bargain

Luke stepped into the tiny jailhouse room reserved for attorney-client meetings, wearing his orange jumpsuit and slip-on sneakers without shoelaces. The guard shut the door behind him.

Gina Walters stood from the metal table, wearing a skirt suit, her dark hair pulled back in a tight bun. "Hello, Mr. Archer."

"Please call me Luke," he replied.

"Of course." She gestured to the chair across from her. "Please sit, Luke. We have a plea bargain to discuss."

They sat across from each other at the table.

Gina continued. "The DA's offering twenty years in prison, no parole, in exchange for a guilty plea. It's a strong offer."

Luke shook his head, his voice quivering. "What about my family? Mary's all alone."

"It's my duty to present any offers I receive from the DA. Whether you take the deal or not is up to you. Either way, it's a positive development. If they believed their case was rock solid, they would've offered to take the death penalty off the table, but you'd still be looking at life in prison."

Luke wrung his hands. "Twenty years might as well be life. I'll miss everything. My daughter won't know me. She'll be an adult by the time I get out of here."

Gina sat ramrod straight, no hint of emotion on her face or in her voice. "Would you like me to decline the offer?"

"What happens if we decline the offer?"

"They might give us a better offer, or we go to trial."

"Do you think we'll get a better offer?"

"I doubt it."

Luke took a deep breath. "If we go to trial, can we win?"

"You're risking your life. If you go to trial and lose, the death penalty is on the table."

"But can we win?"

"It's possible, but, with trials, there are no guarantees."

Luke thought about Mary, alone on their farm, struggling to keep the CSA going, while caring for Abby. "I'd like to go to trial."

CHAPTER 24: CURTIS AND BLM

Over two hundred protesters crowded into Oak Mill Park, about one-half mile from the Carville police station. A group of people handed out premade signs: #BlackLivesMatter. No Justice, No Peace. Silence is Violence. Racism is Small-Dick Energy. Defund the Police. Curtis handed out signs that he'd made too. He dispersed several signs that read, Justice 4 Luke and several that featured a headshot of Officer Bradley Lambert in his police uniform. Under his image read Police Brutality.

A handful of locals were among the protesters, but most of them came from BLM Philly. Surprisingly, the protesters were mostly white and in their twenties. The male-to-female ratio was about equal.

A murmur spread through the crowd of protesters, most of them staring at their phones or sharing their phone screen with another. Amari waded through the crowd toward Curtis, his jaw set tight. He was tall and light-skinned, with defined muscles.

Curtis handed out his last sign to a white woman wearing a BLM T-shirt and a nose ring, his heart pounding as he watched incoming Amari over the woman's shoulder.

Amari stepped very close to Curtis and said through gritted teeth, "We need to talk." He pointed to an open area beyond the parking lot. "Over there."

Curtis followed Amari, like a scolded child, to a lonely patch of grass near the park trailhead. "What's up?" Curtis tried to sound upbeat.

"You lied to me," Amari said, his face hard. "You told me that he was Colombian. He's white. I should've fucking known, with a name like Luke Archer."

Curtis tilted his head and furrowed his brow, giving his best confused impression. "Are you sure? I thought he was part Colombian?"

"Bullshit. You knew what you were doing."

"Does it matter if he's white?"

"What matters is you lied. We're pulling out."

Curtis held out his hands. "Come on, Amari. He saved my life."

Amari shook his head. "That's not what the media's saying."

"You of all people know the media lies."

Amari pointed at Curtis. "All I know is *you* lied." Amari marched back to the crowd of protesters.

Curtis followed a few paces behind.

The crowd was still talking and checking their phones. Curtis caught a glimpse of a woman's screen. It was Luke's mugshot. He did have a tan, but he certainly looked white. *Tisha was right.*

Amari grabbed the megaphone and spoke to the crowd. "Listen up, everybody."

The protesters turned to Amari.

"I'm gonna be straight with you. BLM Philly received faulty information from Justice for Carville, so we're officially pulling out of this event."

The crowd of protesters murmured among themselves.

Someone yelled out, "Dude's white."

Amari held up his hand. "The man's skin color has nothing to do with it. We're exiting this event because we were lied to about important details. Having said that, you are all welcome to march, but please refrain from using BLM signs. Thank you all for coming."

Most of the protesters, including Amari, went to their cars and left, leaving fast-food wrappers, soda cans, and homemade signs strewn about. Curtis tried to stop them, urging them to participate in the march, telling everyone how Luke had saved his life. They ignored Curtis, as if he were a homeless man in the park, begging for change.

Curtis scanned the ten remaining protesters. Most were black and local to Carville, although there were two Latinos, plus a white couple, who looked like sixties-era hippies. The hippies and a few others picked up trash. Curtis joined them, ignoring the dull pain in his back, when he bent over for a piece of trash. Then everyone worked together.

An older woman said, "They come here, make a mess, and leave. Just like my kids at Christmas."

A few laughed at that.

After the cleanup, the ten protesters and Curtis marched toward the police station, their signs in hand. They marched single file through the suburbs on the shoulder of a two-lane road. A few cars honked at them. Curtis wasn't sure if it was in support or opposition. One man yelled something inaudible out the window of his pickup truck, accompanied by his middle finger, which was loud and clear.

As they approached Carville city and the police station, Curtis spotted approximately one hundred protesters already in place. He smiled, thinking that the BLM protesters didn't want to march but were still happy to support the cause. But, as they moved closer, Curtis recognized it for what it was. A counterprotest.

Curtis and his ten supporters marched onto the grass lawn in front of the police station. A handful of police officers stood out front, watching the scene. The counterprotesters surrounded them, holding signs that read Blue Lives Matter, We Love Our Police, and Back the Blue.

The counterprotesters chanted, "Blue lives matter. Blue lives matter."

The protesters with Curtis shouted, "Black lives matter. Black lives matter."

The BLM chants were drowned out by the pro-police crowd.

A dozen police officers pushed through the blue lives matter crowd and surrounded Curtis and his fellow protesters.

A burly officer with sergeant's stripes approached Curtis. He shouted over the chants, "You can't be here."

Curtis shouted back, "This is public property. I'm not leaving."

A few of the other officers quieted the counterprotesters with shouts and hand gestures.

The sergeant addressed Curtis and the ten protesters. "If you don't leave the premises, we'll be forced to arrest you all for disturbing the peace."

"Bullshit," Curtis replied. "It's our First Amendment right to protest. You can't do shit."

"Like I said, we'll arrest you all and let the courts settle it."

"What about them?" Curtis asked, gesturing to the Blue Lives Matter crowd. "They're making a lot more noise than we are."

A hint of a smirk appeared on the sergeant's face. "They'll leave when you leave."

Curtis addressed his fellow protesters. "This is bullshit. We're not going anywhere."

The sergeant let out a heavy breath, then addressed the protesters with Curtis. "You really wanna be arrested for a cop killer? I'll give you five seconds to go home. Five, four, three, two, one."

Most of the protesters lowered their signs and left the area.

The crowd of counterprotesters parted to allow their exit. A few shouted, "Blue lives matter," as they started the half-mile walk of shame back to their cars.

The sergeant nodded to his officers. "Arrest them."

The officers converged on the remaining protesters, Curtis and the hippy couple.

The hippies raised their hands over their heads and said, "We're leaving!"

"Don't leave," Curtis said to the couple's back. "They can't do anything." Curtis reached for his phone, intending to record the interaction, but he forgot that his phone was gone. Immediately after his arraignment, he had requested his phone from the police, assuming they held it in evidence, but they had claimed that they didn't have it. Curtis addressed the sergeant. "I know what you're doing. Go ahead and try to arrest me. I'll sue your punk ass for false arrest."

The sergeant chuckled and walked away, the other officers following. Most of the Blue Lives Matter crowd left too, going to their cars parked in the police station lot.

Twenty or so of the Blue Lives Matter crowd stuck around, tightly surrounding Curtis. They chanted, "Luke Archer. Cop killer. Luke Archer. Cop killer!"

Curtis stood silent, his head held high.

CHAPTER 25: LIZZIE'S NOT ALONE

"Mr. Archer declined the plea deal," District Attorney Alex Perkins said through Lizzie's cell phone.

Lizzie sat on her bed, her legs wobbly, and her stomach turning.

The DA continued. "I'm sorry, Mrs. Lambert. I know you wanted this to be over as soon as possible."

"What happens now?" Lizzie asked.

"We go to trial."

"Is there a chance he could go free?"

"No. Don't worry about that. We have a strong case, with video evidence. He may not get the death penalty, but life in prison is very likely, if not certain."

Lizzie exhaled. "Okay. Thank you, Mr. Perkins."

"You're welcome. I'll be in touch."

Lizzie set her cell phone on her bedside table and lay in the fetal position on her bed. The television was on, but the sound was muted. She gaped at the images on the screen, comatose. It was his name that shot her upright and to the edge of her bed. *Curtis Mays. That black piece of shit.* She was surprised by his youthful appearance, expecting him to look more … *thuggish.* Lizzie unmuted the television. She watched the local news, the male reporter interviewing Curtis, surrounded by police supporters, many with Back the Blue and Blue Lives Matter signs. In the background was the Carville Police Department.

"I'm here because Officer Lambert tried to kill me," Curtis said.

The crowd booed.

Lizzie shouted at the television, "Liar!"

"And Luke Archer's innocent. He did what he had to do to save my life," Curtis said.

The crowd chanted, "Luke Archer. Cop killer. Luke Archer. Cop killer."

Curtis shouted over the crowd into the microphone, "Luke Archer was defending me, and he was defending himself."

The reporter turned to the camera. "For now, Luke Archer remains in jail with a one-million-dollar bond. We'll know more when the preliminary hearing begins next week."

Lizzie dressed in a pair of yoga pants and a T-shirt. She rushed down the hall, passing her mother in the kitchen. She left via the side door, telling her mother, "I'll be back."

"Where are you going?" her mother asked.

Lizzie didn't stop to answer. She hurried to her Ford Explorer and drove toward the Carville Police Department.

When she arrived at the police department, the Channel 7 news van was leaving, along with several other vehicles. Curtis Mays still stood out front, with a sign which included a picture of Brad and the message Police Brutality. Only five men surrounded him now, two holding Blue Lives Matter signs, none of them chanting anymore. Two police officers loitered near the department front door, watching the scene.

Lizzie parked her SUV in the parking lot of the police department. She stalked across the macadam to Curtis and the small group of counter-protesters on the front lawn. She brushed past a heavyset man and came face-to-face with Curtis Mays.

Lizzie put her finger in his face. "You're a goddamn liar!"

Curtis put up his hand. "Get your finger out of my face, lady."

One of the counterprotesters recorded the altercation with his phone.

She continued to stab the air between them, her finger dangerously close to his face. "I'll do whatever the hell I want. It's *your* fault. You got my husband killed. You're a *monster*."

Curtis took a step back. "Your husband tried to kill me. He had some serious anger problems."

"You *asshole*." Lizzie attacked Curtis, slapping him across the face.

Curtis took the first hit without any reaction. He blocked her second attempt with the sign of her dead husband's face.

A muscle-bound police officer grabbed Lizzie around the waist and pulled her away from Curtis.

Lizzie struggled initially, not realizing it was an officer.

"Whoa, Mrs. Lambert," the police officer said.

Lizzie stopped struggling.

"Come on. This isn't a good idea."

The police officer escorted Lizzie into the police station, taking her to Chief Dennis Rhodes's office.

Dennis looked up from his computer. "Lizzie." Dennis stood from his desk and walked toward the open doorway of his office. "What are you doing here?"

"She was in an altercation with that Mays scumbag outside," the muscle-bound police officer said.

Lizzie looked down, embarrassed.

Dennis put up his hand. "I'll handle it from here. Thank you, Gregson."

The officer nodded and left.

Dennis shut the door behind them, giving them privacy. He bent forward, so they were eye to eye. "Are you okay?"

"I don't know."

Dennis put his arm around her and led her to the leather couch. They sat side by side, and Dennis turned toward her. "What's going on?"

Lizzie shrugged, tears welling in her eyes. "I just want this to be over. DA Perkins said Luke Archer turned down the plea deal."

Dennis blew out a breath. "I heard. I'm sorry. Don't worry. We'll get him. We have a strong case."

"That's what Perkins said. He said that life in prison is very likely, if not certain." Lizzie exhaled. "I'm worried that he's just telling me what I want to hear. I'm sorry. I know you two are friends."

"Alex and I do go way back, but I can honestly say that he's the best at what he does. If he's confident, believe it. Don't forget. There's still a chance that Archer will change his mind and realize the plea deal is his best option."

"I hope so." Lizzie sniffled and wiped the corners of her eyes. "I saw Curtis Mays on the news, claiming Archer's innocent, and I just lost it. I went after him, slapped him in the face."

"Well, he had it coming, but you should stay away from him."

Tears slipped down Lizzie's cheeks. "I don't know if I can do this on my own."

Dennis put his large hand on her knee. "You're not alone."

Lizzie nodded, still crying.

Dennis wrapped his arms around her and pulled her to his chest. Lizzie breathed in his musky scent. A man's scent. When she stopped crying, she looked up at Dennis through glassy eyes. That's when he pressed his lips to hers, tentative, straddling the line between friends and lovers. She froze for an instant, but heat spread throughout her body. She reciprocated, with passion, leaving no doubt.

CHAPTER 26: LUKE'S PENANCE

Luke lay in the bottom bunk, his feet dangling over the edge of the tiny bed. He stared at a picture of Mary holding Abby at the farm, dressed in their Sunday best. Tears welled in his eyes, thinking about what he was losing, blurring their beauty. He wiped his eyes, the picture coming back into focus. Mary smiled for the camera, her head haloed by the sun.

Luke had thought of her as an angel from the moment he'd met her at the farmer's market. This was when his parents were still alive. He'd been selling produce from the family farm. Mary had browsed with her sister, wearing a bonnet, her long dress swallowing her petite frame. It was the way she'd smiled at him. The way her face had lit up. Her easy giggle. She'd haggled for the fresh basil. She'd wanted to buy it all, then dry it for future use. He'd practically given it away, with the hope that she'd come back. She did, but she was betrothed to another. Luke pushed the thought from his mind. He didn't want to think about the ugliness with her family.

The light in Luke's cell turned off automatically, casting Mary and Abby in a dark shadow. Dim lights from the hallway provided just enough light to navigate the nine-by-twelve cell. He'd had a cellmate for a few days, a drunk driver, but he was out on bail. Luke rolled out of bed and set the picture on the tiny desktop.

Movement caught the corner of Luke's eye, causing him to check the door window. Luke flinched at the sight of a guard. The lock unlatched with a *clunk*, and the door opened. Two beefy guards entered his cell, causing Luke to step back. They barely fit in the cell side by side. They both held billy clubs. Luke stood with his shoulders slumped and his head bowed.

The one with the thick mustache said, "I heard the DA offered you a pretty sweet deal."

The other one with the crew cut slapped his open palm with his billy club and said, "You should take the deal."

Luke's heart pounded in his chest, his eyes on those sticks. Luke cleared his throat and spoke softly. "I'm going to trial."

The mustachioed guard also slapped his open hand with his billy club and said, "You should rethink that. It's a *big* mistake."

"Yep. *Big* mistake," the crew cut guard agreed.

Luke stood up straight, his shoulders back, towering over the guards. "No. I'm *not* taking that deal."

The mustachioed guard pointed his billy club at Luke. "You'll regret it."

The guards turned and left the cell, but they didn't shut the door. Two large inmates entered the cell single file, almost as big as Luke. One inmate's exposed skin was completely covered in ink. Even his eyelids were tattooed. The other inmate had a shaved head and bulky muscles. The tattooed inmate punched Luke in the jaw, the quickness of the strike catching Luke off guard, and dropping him like a sack of potatoes. Luke fell awkwardly, his right shoulder hitting the edge of the bottom bunk, pain radiating from his jaw.

Luke's vision blurred. The room spun. The tattooed inmate kicked Luke in the stomach. Luke gasped for breath as the wind was knocked out of him. Then the bald inmate joined in, kicking and stomping Luke with his feet. Luke pulled himself into a tight fetal position, covering his head with his arms.

The kicks kept coming, but Luke didn't fight back. It was his penance.

CHAPTER 27: CURTIS AND PROVE IT

For the second day in a row, Curtis paced on the front lawn of the Carville police station, holding his sign, picturing Officer Lambert with the message Police Brutality. The grass was matted where he'd been picketing back and forth. The counterprotesters had left yesterday, shortly after his argument with Lambert's wife. They hadn't been back since.

The bright sun warmed his skin. A police car turned into the station, the officer mean-mugging Curtis through the open cruiser window on the way to the parking lot. Curtis waved back, as if they were best buds.

Shortly thereafter, Tisha's little red Honda pulled into the department parking lot. She walked toward Curtis, holding a bottled water. Curtis stopped pacing and faced his girlfriend.

Tisha held out the bottled water. "I thought you might be thirsty."

Curtis set down his sign and took the plastic bottle. "Thanks."

Tisha nodded.

"You want a sign?" Curtis asked, opening the cap on the water bottle.

"I'm not here for that."

Curtis took a swig of water. "Why are you here then?"

Tisha put her hands on her curvy hips. "What if he's guilty of murder?"

"What if he's not? What if he risked his life and his freedom for a black man he's never met?"

Tisha laughed, but it wasn't jovial. "When was the last time a white man risked anything for us?"

"There was a white couple at the protest yesterday."

Tisha held out her hands. "Where are they now?"

"The police ..."

"Let me guess. As soon as shit got real, they bounced."

65

Curtis looked away for a beat.

Tisha took his free hand and squeezed. "I'm not trying to be a bitch, but, if you want my help with this, it has to be relevant to our community. When we started Justice for Carville, it was supposed to be for *our* community. It can't just be justice for Luke Archer."

"It's not," Curtis replied. "This is *very* relevant to everyone in Carville."

Tisha retracted her hand from his. "Prove it." She walked away, back toward her car.

"I will," Curtis called out to her back.

Curtis watched Tisha and her red Honda drive away from the police station. Curtis chugged the rest of the water, then walked to his backpack, and slipped the empty bottle inside. He returned to his sign and his picketing.

As he paced back and forth, he thought about Tisha's words. *She's wrong. This is about Luke Archer, but it's also about everyone in Carville. The police may not be killing innocent people on the regular, but they are abusing their power. Excessive fines for bullshit regulations. Police brutality.*

A car honked. Curtis ignored the car, no longer making eye contact with the angry faces who often initiated the honks.

I have to prove that Luke was justified. Tisha's right that this can't be just about Luke though. To really change things, I have to prove that the Carville police are abusing their power as policy, that it's not just one bad egg. And I have to figure out a way to get that information to every single resident in Carville.

Curtis stopped pacing, an idea forming in his mind. *I need budget information. Historical crime stats. Everything about the police I can find. The county office should have that stuff.*

CHAPTER 28: LIZZIE AND VIRAL

Over the past twenty-four hours, since her argument with Curtis Mays, and the kiss she'd shared with Dennis, Lizzie had stayed in her bedroom. Yesterday evening, her phone had buzzed constantly with texts and phone calls, many of those calls coming from her best friend, Julie. Lizzie worried that Dennis had told his wife about the kiss, and she wasn't ready to face the music, so she'd turned off her phone.

A knock came on her bedroom door. "Do you want some lunch?" Helen asked through the locked door.

Lizzie raised her head from her pillow and called back to her mother, "No thanks."

There was a long pause, then Helen said, "You should really check your phone. There's a video on the internet."

Lizzie frowned. "A what?"

"Just check your phone." Helen walked away.

Lizzie exhaled and grabbed her phone from her bedside table. As her phone powered on, she thought about how to respond to Julie. *Apologetic? I'm so sorry, Julie. I'm such an emotional mess. Dennis hugged me, and it just happened. It didn't mean anything.* Lizzie pursed her lips. *It really is Dennis's fault. Maybe that's what I should tell her?*

Lizzie wondered how far it would've gone had she not left abruptly after the kiss. She imagined having sex with Dennis on that leather couch. Straddling him. Feeling his large hands all over her body. His mouth on her nipples. Feeling him inside her.

Her phone powered on and immediately buzzed with another text, waking her from her daydream. She had twenty-four missed calls and even more texts. She opened Julie's text's first, wanting to bite the bullet.

Julie: Hi Lizzie. I hope you're doing okay. I'm worried about you. Not sure if you've seen this video of you but it's going viral. Most of the comments are supporting you which is good. Dennis told me to tell you to make sure to stay away from Curtis Mays from now on. If you need me for anything let me know and I'll be there in a flash. I love you. Here's a link to the video if you haven't seen it. **Link**

Lizzie tapped the link and watched a replay of the slap and her argument with Curtis Mays. The video had been viewed on Facebook over one million times. She cringed at that, not proud of her behavior and especially not proud of her messy hair and lack of makeup. She read a few Facebook comments.

Jeff Sills

Dude blocked her with her dead husband's face. That's cold.

Alice A.

What a creep! Her husband is dead and he's complaining about police brutality. This is why everyone hates BLM.

Harry the Great

Blue Lives Matter!

Reggie Robinson

From what I read, the cop did knock that man unconscious. The sign looks pretty accurate to me.

Vinson Ray

BS. He was resisting, like they always do

Gayle Trudeau

Why can't people just listen to the police? Everybody would be a lot better off.

CHAPTER 29: MARY AND THE LETTUCE

On Friday morning, Mary went outside to check the crops, the baby monitor in her pocket. As she approached the rows of vegetables, a sick feeling came from deep in the pit of her stomach.

She rushed over to the long row of lettuce, which was due for harvest soon. She bent down and touched the brown and dried lettuce leaves. Most of the plants were still alive, but none of the crop was salable. She ran to the shed, raised the rollup door, and grabbed the jug of neem oil concentrate. She checked the label, sure she had followed the instructions. Then she found her mistake.

> As with other oil-based products, exercise care in timing applications to early morning/late evening to minimize the potential for leaf burn.

Mary put her head in her hands. Then Abby's cries came through the baby monitor.

CHAPTER 30: CURTIS AND LEGAL THEFT

Curtis sat at a round wooden table in the Carville County offices. He scoured stacks of budgetary and finance documents, taking notes. He said to himself, "They're broke."

The middle-aged woman at the counter said, "Excuse me?"

Curtis showed his palms. "Sorry. I was thinking out loud."

She smiled and went back to her work.

Curtis read his notes, thinking about the implications. *In 2001, the county had less than three million dollars in debt. Now they owe eighteen million. Twenty years ago, 9 percent of the revenue came from fines, fees, and asset forfeiture. Last year it was 38 percent. We're on track for 42 percent this year. Nonmoving violations have tripled since 2001. Code violations have quadrupled.* Curtis looked up from his notes. He tapped his lips, still thinking. *Instead of raising taxes or cutting expenses, they're using fines and tickets to fund the government. It's legal theft.*

Curtis returned the documents, grabbed his notebook, and left the county office. He fast-walked through town toward home, rain clouds threatening, passing dilapidated rowhomes. He wondered how many residents had had their lives destroyed because they couldn't afford to pay their fines to Carville County. A simple ticket could be the difference between eating or the light bill. An unpaid ticket could lead to a suspended license. A suspended license could lead to a job loss. A job loss could lead to a foreclosure or an eviction. An eviction could lead to homelessness.

His new cell phone chimed in his pocket. Curtis answered his phone and was greeted by his public defender, Hugh Ellis.

"I have good news," Hugh said. "The DA's offering six months in prison and a $5,000 fine if you plead guilty."

Curtis frowned, still fast-walking, hoping to beat the rain. "I already told you that I'm not taking a deal. I'm innocent, and the bodycam footage will show that."

"What if I could get them to give you probation, no jail time?"

"I'd still have a record, and I'd be on probation for a year or longer. Then, if I make one mistake, they send me to jail, right?"

"It depends on the mistake."

Curtis spoke through gritted teeth. "I'm *not* pleading guilty."

"You could plead no contest."

"*No*. In fact, I should be suing *them*."

Hugh let out a heavy breath. "The commonwealth doesn't like going to trial. It's not uncommon for judges to impose max penalties and to run sentences for multiple charges consecutively. That might mean four years in prison for you. You really want to take that risk?"

"No deal." Curtis hung up the phone.

Raindrops fell from the sky.

CHAPTER 31: LUKE AND THE LAST REFUGE OF A SCOUNDREL

Two guards escorted Luke from sick bay toward the cells. Luke walked gingerly down the hall, his back and ribs aching, and his hands cuffed in front of him.

Luke was uncuffed once they were back in the jail common area, which resembled an indoor courtyard, surrounded by cells, with stainless-steel tables and chairs bolted to the floor. A handful of guards patrolled the perimeter. A few prisoners gawked at Luke, but nobody said anything. Luke trudged back to his cell and kneeled before his bottom bunk, the unforgiving concrete biting his kneecaps. He closed his eyes and clasped his hands together. His lips moved with his prayer, but he didn't make a sound.

God, if I have forsaken You, I will accept my just punishment. If that means a lifetime in prison, I will accept Your will. Please help Mary and Abby. They don't deserve to be punished for my sins. Please, God. Help them.

CHAPTER 32: LIZZIE'S LOSING IT

Rain peppered the asphalt shingles of her home. Lizzie sat on her couch in a trance, watching Ellen DeGeneres do her goofy dance, the audience howling with laughter. Brian played with his muscle-bound action figures on the living room carpet. Emma played with her dolls. Brian made gun noises, aiming the rifle of one of his men at Emma's dolls.

"She's dead," Brian said.

"*Nuh-uh*. You can't do that. I'm not even playing with you," Emma replied.

Brian snatched the doll from Emma and placed it facedown on the carpet. "Sometimes people die."

Emma sniffled.

Lizzie snapped to attention. "*Brian*. Give her back her doll. *Now*."

Brian picked up the doll and stared at it for an instant. Then he ripped it's head off and tossed it to Emma. "*Dead*. Just like Dad."

Emma wailed.

Lizzie sprang from the couch and grabbed Brian by his shirt collar. She smacked him across the face. "Don't you *ever* do something like that again."

Brian put his hand to his cheek. His face reddened, and he burst into tears.

Lizzie's mother, Helen, rushed into the living room from the kitchen.

Brian ran to Helen, hugging her waist.

"*What* is going on?" Helen asked, glaring at Lizzie.

Lizzie opened her mouth to speak, but nothing came out.

"Mommy hit me," Brian said, blubbering into Helen's dress.

Emma held out her decapitated doll to Helen, tears streaming down her face. "Brian killed Molly."

Helen bent down to Brian, her hands on his cheeks, checking his face. "Are you hurt, honey?"

He sniffed and shook his head.

"You need to say *sorry* to your sister."

He bowed his head and said, "Sorry."

"Go in the kitchen. If you help me with dinner, I'll make you a treat."

Brian trudged to the kitchen, swiping one of his action figures from the floor before he left.

Helen went to Emma and hugged the little girl. Then she pulled back and said, "Let's fix Molly."

Emma pouted and said, "Can't fix dead."

"I can fix it," Lizzie interjected.

Emma turned her back to Lizzie, hugged her doll to her chest, and said, "*No.*"

"Give Molly to me, honey. Grammys can fix anything," Helen said.

Emma handed the doll to her grammy.

Helen grabbed the head from the floor, reattached it to the doll, and handed it back to Emma. "All better. She's got her head on straight now."

Emma took the doll and smiled.

"Why don't you take your dolls to your room, honey?"

Emma gathered her dolls and left the living room.

Helen put her hands on her hips and narrowed her eyes at Lizzie.

"*What?*" Lizzie replied.

Helen spoke in a sharp whisper. "You need to get your shit together."

CHAPTER 33: CURTIS AND LUKE

Polycarbonate "glass" separated Curtis from Luke Archer at the Carville County Jail. The men stared at each other for a long beat. Luke had bruising along his jawline. The men grabbed their phone receivers.

"You're Curtis Mays," Luke said, remembering his name from his police interview.

Curtis nodded. "I, uh, ..."

"What do you want?"

Curtis took a deep breath. "I, ... I wanted to thank you for what you did for me. I didn't see it. I was unconscious, but I heard about what happened. You saved my life. If you hadn't stepped in, I'd be dead." Curtis dipped his head. "I know a *thank you* won't get you out of here, but thank you."

Luke shrugged. "No offense, but I'm not sure I did the right thing. A man's dead, and I'm in here."

"I don't know if you know this, but Officer Lambert was beating me because he was pissed that I was filming his traffic stop. He would've beaten me to death if you hadn't come along. Believe that." Curtis gazed into Luke's eyes. "You damn sure did the right thing."

"God will judge me."

An awkward silence passed between them.

"Is that what you came to tell me?" Luke asked.

"Partly. I'd like to help you in any way I can. I marched for you in front of the police station. I plan to do more. I run a nonprofit called Justice for Carville. I'm a professional activist. Hopefully, I can sway public opinion in your favor. That might help with your trial."

Luke rubbed the stubble on his chin, unimpressed with Curtis's activism. "You really want to help me?"

Curtis leaned forward. "Yes."

"You ever farm?"

CHAPTER 34: MARY BURNS THE MIDNIGHT OIL

Raindrops pelted Mary's raincoat. She picked muddy radishes in the dark, using Luke's headlamp. She removed a rubber band from her wrist, tied a bundle of six radishes, and dropped them in her crate. She continued along the row, leaving a full crate every twenty feet or so.

She had been harvesting various crops on and off for sixteen hours, taking multiple breaks to care for Abby. Once Mary had harvested and washed the crops, she carried forty-three crates brimming with produce into the kitchen and dining room. She glanced at the clock on her stove—*3:37 a.m.*

Inside, she removed her raincoat and muck boots, then washed her hands, scrubbing away the dirt under her nails. Her fingertips were wrinkled from the rain. She set Abby's monitor on the table and went to work, preparing the CSA baskets. Half of the baskets had to be delivered by noon on Saturday. The other half were due at noon on Sunday. It wasn't uncommon for their customers to be waiting at their drop-off points before noon.

Mary spread out all 147 of the empty boxes throughout the kitchen, dining room, and living room. Then she added a bit of each crop into each box. How much to add was a bit of a science and a bit of an art. She estimated how much she had of each crop, then did a little math to get an estimate of how much to put in each box. It was always preferable to have a little left over. As she separated the produce, she threw out anything diseased or damaged.

She worked at a feverish pace, adrenaline keeping her awake. Thankfully, apart from Abby's breathing, her baby monitor stayed quiet.

***

Sunshine slipped between the blinds in the kitchen. Mary surveyed the neatly packed boxes, her vision blurry. *I did it. Thank God.* Abby's cries came from the baby monitor. Mary went to her daughter and fed her. She dozed in the rocking chair, as Abby breastfed. Mary jolted awake when Abby cried, having unlatched from her breast. Mary fed her again, then burped her and changed her diaper. She set Abby back in her crib and turned on the mobile, the little bears dancing round and round.

Mary's feet and lower back ached. She inspected her hands and her green-stained fingertips. The room spun around her. Mary sat in the rocking chair again, intending to rest her aches and pains, knowing she'd need to get ready for the deliveries soon. She closed her eyes. In an instant, she was gone.

***

Knocking came from somewhere. Mary's eyes fluttered and opened. Sun shone between the blinds. Mary shot upright. She thought, *Oh, no. What time is it?*

More knocking came from her side door.

Mary checked Abby. She was awake but seemingly content. Mary rushed to the kitchen and the side door, checking the clock on the stove. It was 11:21 a.m.

A young black man stood at her door window. He was tall and lean, with short hair and a baby face. He saw her notice him, and he waved. But she didn't know a single black person. She went to the door tentatively and talked through the window.

"Can I help you?" Mary discreetly turned the lock on the doorknob.

"I'm Curtis Mays."

Mary scowled, recognizing his name as the man partly responsible for her husband's predicament.

Curtis continued. "I spoke with your husband. He said you might need help with some farm work."

Mary opened the door, the scowl still on her face. "We don't have any money."

Curtis showed his palms. "I don't want your money. I'd like to help you. I've done a lot of landscaping with my dad."

Mary crossed her arms over her chest.

Curtis narrowed his eyes at Mary. "Are you okay, Mrs. Archer? You look … really tired."

Abby cried through the baby monitor on the kitchen table.

Mary leaned against the doorframe, her head hanging, and tears welling in her eyes. "I'll never make it."

"Never make what?"

Mary shook her head.

"Your husband said you might need some help delivering the produce today. I have a truck."

Mary stood and peered over Curtis's shoulder, his pickup truck catching her eye. She wiped the corners of her eyes and said, "You're a godsend."

CHAPTER 35: LIZZIE AND DENNIS

Lizzie sat at the head of the table, pushing peas around her plate, her phone facedown on the table. Helen sat at the foot of the table, near the children, cutting Emma's hot dog into bite-size pieces. Brian sat on the other side of Helen, purposely eating his hot dog with his mouth open.

"Gross," Emma said, pointing at her brother.

"Mouth closed, Brian," Helen said.

Brian grinned and closed his mouth.

Lizzie's phone buzzed. She checked her texts.

> **Dennis:** I need to see you.

Lizzie texted back.

> **Lizzie:** When

> **Dennis:** In 20 min. Oak Mill Park.

> **Lizzie:** Ok

Lizzie stood from the table and grabbed her plate. "Thanks for lunch, Mom. I need to run to the store for a few things."

"I bought groceries yesterday," Helen replied.

"I need a few things. I won't be long." Lizzie stared at her children for a moment, half hoping for a protest or a request for her speedy return, but nothing.

Lizzie dumped her food into the trash and went to her bedroom. She checked herself in the mirror and frowned. Her hair was disheveled. Her face was washed-out, and her T-shirt had a stain. She felt the urge to shower and to put on a dress with chunky heels, but she didn't have time. So she changed her sports bra for something white and lacy, and she put on a clean T-shirt. She put on deodorant and perfume. She fixed her hair and quickly put on some eyeliner and lip gloss.

Then she rushed out the side door, careful not to let her mother see her, or Helen might wonder why Lizzie had put on makeup for the first time since the funeral.

Lizzie drove across Carville to Oak Mill Park in eleven minutes. A half-dozen cars were in the lot. Two people loitered at the trailhead, fixing their backpacks. Dennis's police SUV was parked toward the back of the lot. Lizzie parked next to him, the sun in her face. Dennis exited his vehicle and climbed into the passenger seat of Lizzie's Ford Explorer.

"Thank you for coming," Dennis said, looking her up and down.

"Of course. What did you need to talk about?" Lizzie replied, knowing full well he didn't mention anything about talking.

Dennis surveyed the parking lot. "Let's get out of here."

Lizzie drove, while Dennis navigated, telling her when and where to turn. They didn't talk during the short trip to an unfamiliar gravel road, but Lizzie's stomach fluttered, anticipating what was to come.

"Where are we going?" Lizzie asked, her tires crunching the gravel.

"You'll see," Dennis replied.

The gravel road took them into the wilderness for a few hundred yards, tree branches scraping the sides of Lizzie's SUV.

Dennis pointed at a chain up ahead that spanned the width of the road. "Stop up there."

She stopped the Ford Explorer at the chain. A sign hung from the chain that read Private Property.

"I'll be right back." Dennis got out of the truck, went to the chain, unlocked it, and set it aside. He waved Lizzie through.

Once Lizzie drove through the gate, Dennis reset the chain, and locked it behind them. Then they drove another two hundred yards and parked at a dead end.

"This is an old logging trail," Dennis said.

Lizzie nodded, staring at the forest.

Dennis opened the passenger door. "Come on. I have something to show you."

They walked single file through the dense woods, with Dennis leading the way. A squirrel darted away from them and climbed an oak tree faster than Lizzie could run on flat ground. A small log cabin appeared in the distance.

Dennis pointed to the cabin, with a detached outhouse. "That's my hunting camp. I don't hunt much these days though."

"It's quiet," Lizzie said, scanning the forest for any sign of civilization, and finding none.

Dennis glanced over his shoulder and grinned. "I thought you could use a little quiet away from the world."

Lizzie forced a smile back. She thought about telling Dennis that she wanted to go home, but she kept putting one foot in front of the other, following him like a puppy.

Dennis led them to the front door. Firewood was stacked on the porch. Dennis unlocked the dead bolt and opened the door, letting Lizzie in first.

It was nearly dark, only the dappled sun from the forest canopy providing light. The one-room cabin had a double bed, small kitchen, fireplace, and an old couch.

Dennis shut the door, darkening the room further. He lit a few candles, setting them on the coffee table by the couch. He gestured to the couch. "Have a seat."

Lizzie sat on the edge of it.

"You want something to drink?" Dennis walked to the kitchen and opened the cooler on the table. "I have some wine. I think it's the stuff that you and ... that you like to drink."

Lizzie knew he was about to say, *you and Julie*. Nothing kills the mood quite like mentioning his wife and her best friend. "Wine sounds good."

Dennis opened the bottle of wine and poured a generous glass for Lizzie. He opened a beer for himself and brought the beverages to the couch. He handed the glass of wine to Lizzie and sat next to her.

She wondered if he wanted to toast. *What the hell would we toast?*

He guzzled half his beer in one long swig.

She took a large gulp of her wine.

Dennis set his beer on the coffee table. "Can I be honest with you?"

"Of course."

"I've had feelings for you since we first met."

"You have?" Lizzie set her wineglass on the coffee table.

Dennis blushed and nodded. "I'm sorry. I know I must be coming off like a huge asshole."

"No. I'm glad you told me."

Dennis let out a breath. "What about you?"

"What about me?"

"I mean, … I thought, after the other day, you had feelings for me too. Am I wrong about that?"

She shook her head. Then she took another gulp of her wine and placed the glass back on the coffee table. "We shouldn't."

"I know."

"Julie would be devastated."

Dennis hung his head and said, "Julie doesn't love me anymore."

Lizzie furrowed her brow. "That's not true."

"You might be her best friend, but she doesn't tell you everything."

"What are you talking about?"

Dennis rubbed his eyes and raised his gaze to meet Lizzie's. "You know our history. We've been trying for a baby for ten years. It's over. We're not trying anymore. A few months ago, she told me that our marriage isn't enough without a child."

"She's just upset. That's all. You could always adopt."

Dennis shook his head. "When I asked her if she still loved me, she said she didn't think so. Adopting a child into a loveless marriage won't fix it."

"I'm sorry."

Dennis shrugged. "It is what it is."

"What about divorce?"

Dennis shrugged again. "It's a possibility."

Lizzie nodded.

"I'm sorry, Lizzie. I shouldn't have brought you here." Dennis stood from the couch. "Let's forget all about this."

Lizzie reached out and took his thick hand, her heart pounding. "What if I don't want to?" She stood from the couch and looked up at him.

He inched closer, their bodies touching. He cupped her face and pressed his lips to hers. When they separated, Lizzie unbuttoned his police shirt, the badge glinting in the candlelight.

He kissed her neck, breathing in her scent, then stepped back. "You smell so good." He finished the final button for Lizzie, removed his shirt, then removed his undershirt too.

She stepped forward and touched his hairy barrel chest with both hands. He was bulky but solid, like a bear. Dennis reached behind her shirt and unclasped her bra. Then he tugged her T-shirt upward, exposing her midriff. She stepped back, biting her lower lip. Their shadows were projected on the wall by candlelight. She removed her shirt and bra, exposing her breasts. She kicked off her shoes and slipped off her socks. He did the same, slipping off his black leather shoes and removing his socks. He leered at her, as she slid her yoga pants and underwear down her legs together, until she stepped out of the tiny pile of clothes, naked as the day she was born.

He was stunned.

Lizzie smiled in the candlelight. "You okay?"

"I've never seen someone more beautiful."

Lizzie blushed and gestured to his pants. "You're not finished."

Dennis unbuckled his pants, letting them fall to the floor, exposing his boxer briefs and an obvious erection. Lizzie watched his crotch as he removed his briefs. Then they were pawing at each other, with their mouths and their hands. They kissed urgently, their teeth clicking together in the ferocity. His hand was between her legs. Hers gripped his erection.

Lizzie pushed him back to the couch, forcing him to sit down. She straddled him, lifting up, allowing him to place the head of his penis into position. Then she lowered herself onto him, moaning as each inch of him filled her.

He gasped, his hands on her hips.

She wrapped her arms around him, moving her hips back and forth, like waves. He moved with her in rhythm, their heavy breathing in sync. They rode the waves for several minutes to the crescendo. Lizzie gazed into his eyes, rubbing her clitoris against him, while he pushed deep inside her. She moved faster, harder.

He grimaced and said, "Slow down. I'm close."

"So am I." She let out a long moan, her vagina contracting and slickening.

This sent Dennis into a frenzy, his penis spasming inside her. After their shared climax, she rested her head on his shoulder. He wrapped his arms around her and squeezed.

"Wow," he said.

"Wow," she said.

Chapter 36: Curtis and You Know How They Are

Curtis mowed the front yard of a middle unit townhouse on Grange Court, striping up the postage-stamp-size lawn in less than two minutes. His father followed a few houses behind him trimming, edging, and blowing off the sidewalks. The recent rain and the typical hectic spring had put his father behind schedule. Curtis had agreed to help his father that Monday.

It had been ten days since he'd been beaten by Officer Lambert. His back was mostly healed, only light bruising still visible.

Curtis noted that their client occupied the third house from the end of the row. He walked behind the self-propelled mower, guiding it to the backyard, cutting through two unfenced yards to the client's fenced yard. He opened the rear gate and entered the yard. A dog barked from inside the house.

A woman wearing a purple muumuu stood on the second-floor deck, staring down at Curtis, her arms crossed over her chest.

Curtis smiled and waved, but the woman didn't move a muscle. He mowed the lawn, watching his step for potential land mines, but he still stepped in two, the soft mounds spreading and sticking to his boots. In addition to the dog shit, six straight hours of breathing the fumes from the old two-cycle mower had Curtis fighting a headache.

On the way out, the woman shouted at Curtis. Between his ear protection and the roar of the mower, her words were inaudible. Curtis throttled down the mower, took off his ear protection, and returned to the open gate. "Yes, ma'am?"

The middle-aged woman scowled. "Aren't you gonna finish? The edges are long."

The mower was unable to cut the grass that grew tight to the fence.

84

Curtis forced a smile. "My dad will get it. He does the trimming. He's about thirty minutes behind me. It's more efficient if—"

The woman turned and went back inside.

Curtis huffed and guided the mower, again cutting across the backyards of two neighbors. When he rounded the corner, an older white man stood there, with his jaw set tight and one hand held up, like a stop sign. Curtis throttled down the mower again, took off his ear protection, and smiled at the man. It wasn't uncommon for potential customers to stop him while he was working.

The older man gestured to the grass behind Curtis. "You need to stay off my lawn. You're gonna leak gasoline with that old mower and kill my grass."

"My mower's not leaking any fuel."

"I don't care. Stay off my lawn."

Curtis flashed his palms. "No problem."

Curtis left the property, walking behind his mower. He reached into his pocket, removing a folded, stapled set of papers. He checked the route, noting the next few nearby houses. He walked down the street and mowed the yards for seven more townhouses.

Forty-five minutes later, he returned to Grange Court, searching for his father. Leonard's Chevy 2500 was parked in a visitor's space. A police car was parked behind the pickup, blocking him in. Leonard stood on the sidewalk, talking to a police officer and the old man who had accosted Curtis less than an hour ago.

As Curtis approached the scene, he noticed the police officer inspecting his father's keys.

The officer handed the keys back to Leonard and said, "They're clean."

The old man pointed at Curtis. "Check that one. I bet he was the one."

Curtis parked his mower next to the truck and cut the engine. He approached his father and the police officer, his face twisted in annoyance. "All I did was walk on the man's lawn."

"He's sayin' we keyed his car," Leonard said.

"You have any keys on you?" the police officer asked.

"That's none of your business," Curtis replied.

"I knew it," the old man said.

Leonard gave Curtis a look. "Just show him your keys, son."

"This is bullshit. I didn't key his car," Curtis said.

"Then you shouldn't have any blue paint on your keys," the police officer replied.

"That's not the point. You can't search me without a warrant."

"I'm not trying to search you, sir. I'm trying to resolve this dispute."

"Please, son," Leonard said. "Show 'em your keys, so we can get up outta here. I don't have time to argue about this. We still got twenty more houses."

Curtis blew out a breath and reached into his pocket. "This is some bullshit." He handed his key ring to the police officer, which consisted of a spare key to the truck and his house key.

The police officer inspected each key, holding them up, and squinting at the metal. He handed the keys back to Curtis and said to the old man, "They're clean."

"He must've wiped them off," the old man said.

Curtis frowned at the man. "You can't be for real."

"Are you sure the damage to your car just happened?" the police officer asked.

"It had to be them," the old man said. "You know how they are."

"What do you mean by *they*?" Curtis asked.

Leonard put his hand on Curtis's shoulder. "Leave it alone."

"You two are free to go," the police officer said.

"We were always free to go because we didn't do anything," Curtis replied.

"That's *enough*." Leonard escorted Curtis to the passenger door. "Get in the truck."

Curtis climbed into the truck, slamming the door behind him, a hint of dog shit lingering from his boots.

Leonard loaded the mower in the back by tilting it up on one wheel, then hooking a wheel on the tailgate, hauling it up to two wheels, and rolling it into the bed. Leonard shut the tailgate and climbed into the truck with Curtis. The police officer talked to the old man on the sidewalk, the cruiser still blocking their exit.

"He needs to move his car," Curtis said.

"You gotta stop with the attitude," Leonard replied. "This is my business. My reputation means somethin'."

"I don't know how you do this every day. Some of these people treat us like shit."

"That's the nature of the service business."

"They act like we're their slaves."

Leonard shook his head. "It ain't like that, son. They hired me to do a job. I agreed to do the job. I can quit anytime I want, and they can fire me anytime they want."

CHAPTER 37: MARY AND THE SHUNNING

The sun shone with nary a cloud, while Mary pushed the two-wheel seeder along the row, planting sweet corn. The contraption had a little plow that cut a furrow in the soil at the proper depth. As the wheels turned, the hopper dropped one seed into the furrow every twenty inches. A chain hung from the machine, dragging on the loose soil and covering the furrow automatically after planting.

At the end of the row, she turned to watch Curtis harvesting the last of the radishes, using rubber bands to put them in bunches, just like Mary had taught him. Abby cried through the baby monitor in the front pocket of Mary's overalls.

Mary called out to Curtis, "I'll be back. Abby's crying."

He waved in response.

Mary went inside and breastfed Abby, rocking in her late mother-in-law's rocking chair. After feeding Abby, Mary burped her daughter and brought her outside in her covered stroller. Mary pushed the stroller into the greenhouse, rolling on the plastic woven fabric that covered the bare ground, preventing weeds and mud. She found Curtis at the wash station, cleaning the root vegetables. The mechanical fans hummed in the background, dispelling the hot air, and replacing it with a cool breeze.

"She's up," Curtis said, smiling at Abby, sucking her pacifier.

"I've been blessed. She's a good little sleeper."

Curtis nodded.

"You're a fast worker," Mary said, handing a bunch of beets to Curtis to wash.

Curtis took the beets. "It's probably from working with my dad. We mowed like fifty houses the other day." He placed the beets into the crate.

Mary handed him another bunch. "Thank you. I'm grateful for all your help. I know Luke's grateful too."

Curtis smiled, not taking his eyes off his work. "You're welcome. I'm glad I can help."

Abby spit out her pacifier, then grunted her displeasure. Mary retrieved the pacifier from the ground, reached over Curtis, and washed it in the running water. "Excuse my reach."

"You're okay," Curtis replied.

Mary popped the pacifier back into Abby's mouth, then stood next to Curtis again. "So, is it just you and your dad? Do you have any brothers or sisters?"

"It's just me and my dad. My mother left us a long time ago. I have an older brother, but he's in prison upstate. Drug possession. His third offense."

"Oh, I'm sorry." Mary handed him a bunch of purple-top turnips.

Curtis shrugged and took the turnips. "He's not a criminal. He's an addict. It's one of the reasons I started my nonprofit." Curtis washed the turnips unnecessarily long, then tossed them in the crate. "The justice system is a business." Curtis put up air quotes when he said *justice*. "I did some research the other day on the budget for Carville County. In 2001, 9 percent of their revenue came from fines, fees, and asset forfeiture. Now it's like 42 percent."

"What's asset forfeiture?" Mary handed him another bunch of turnips.

"It's basically when the police steal your stuff. If you get caught with drugs in your car, the police can take your car and any money you have on you. Basically, they can take any asset that they think was purchased with criminal activity or used as part of a crime."

"As long as you're not committing a crime—"

"I know plenty of people who had their money stolen and were never charged with a crime." Curtis tossed the turnips in the crate. "It happened to my barber. He had a bunch of cash from work. The cops thought it was too much. Claimed it was from the drug trade. They never charged him, but they took his money. He could've hired a lawyer to get it back, but he would've paid more in legal fees than they took."

Mary handed him the final bunch of turnips. "I didn't know they could do that."

Curtis washed the produce. "They can and they do. Instead of making budget cuts or raising taxes, they're using fines, tickets, and asset forfeiture to make up the budget deficits. It's legal theft." Curtis shut off the water, tossed the turnips into the crate, and turned to Mary. "Did you know that if you add up all the property cops steal through asset forfeiture in the US, it's more than all the burglaries?"

"I had no idea."

"I'm working on a video about this for my YouTube channel. I need to find some people who'll talk though. Not too many people around here want to piss off the cops."

"I can understand that."

Curtis grabbed three crates, stacked on top of each other. "These go in the root cellar, right?"

"That's right. Let's use the cart though." Mary pulled the four-wheel wagon from the corner of the greenhouse to the wash area.

Curtis and Mary stacked the crates on the cart, then Curtis pulled the cart outside. Mary led the way, pushing the stroller to a nearby mound, with a small door, and pipes protruding from the mound. She opened the door, revealing steps down.

Curtis and Mary descended the steps to the earthen root cellar, carrying crates of root vegetables. Abby stayed aboveground, strapped into the stroller. The underground air was noticeably cooler and more humid.

As they stacked crates on the plastic shelves, Curtis asked, "Where did you meet Luke?"

Mary turned to Curtis. "We met at a farmer's market."

"That makes sense."

"I guess it is, what's the word? ... Cliché?"

He grimaced. "I didn't mean it like that."

"It's okay. I'm not offended."

They exited the root cellar, climbing the steps. Abby still sucked her pacifier, her eyes heavy. They grabbed a few more crates from the cart and returned to the root cellar.

"I used to be Amish," Mary said, as she hefted a crate on a shelf.

Curtis set two stacked crates on a shelf and turned to Mary. "Really?"

She nodded. "I was supposed to marry someone else. A son of someone important in the Amish community."

Curtis arched his eyebrows. "But you married Luke."

"I married Luke."

"What happened with the other guy? Was he mad?"

"No. I don't think he really cared. His parents did though, and so did mine."

"What happened?"

"I, ... I was—" Mary's voice caught. She looked away for a moment, then turned back to Curtis. "Sorry. ... I was shunned."

CHAPTER 38: LIZZIE AND HER BEST EFFORT

Lizzie trudged down the hall to the kitchen, still wearing her pajamas. Helen sat at the kitchen table, reading a romance novel, a cup of coffee on the table.

Helen glanced at the clock on the oven and said, "It's alive."

It was after ten in the morning.

Lizzie went straight to the coffeepot and poured herself a cup. She added creamer and sugar. As she stirred her coffee, she said, "Did the kids get off to school okay?"

Helen sighed and set her paperback on the table faceup, revealing a bare-chested and muscle-bound man. "They were fine. They'd be better if *you* were at breakfast."

Lizzie turned from the counter to face her mother, her coffee cup in hand. "I'm doing the best I can."

Helen rolled her eyes.

"What was that?" Lizzie asked.

Helen shook her head. "Nothing."

Lizzie stepped closer to her mother. "You rolled your eyes at me. Obviously, you think I'm *not* doing the best I can."

"It's not for me to say."

"It's *not*? That would be a first for you."

"Don't be disrespectful."

Lizzie set her coffee on the kitchen table, sat across from her mother, and glared. "When have you *ever* shut up about anything?"

"Fine. I was trying to be understanding, but, if you want the truth, I'll give you the unvarnished truth." Helen paused for a second. "You're *not* being a mother to your children. All you do is sleep. When you're not sleeping, you disappear for hours on end."

"What are you talking about? I'm always here."

"What about last Saturday? You said you were going to the store, that you'd be right back, but you were gone for three hours, and you came back with nothing. Where'd you go?"

"I don't have to answer to you. I'm an adult. This is *my* house. Who the *hell* do you think you are?"

Helen pursed her lips. "I'm the person who's been caring for your children, while you do God knows what with God knows who."

Lizzie twisted her face in anger. "Don't act all high and mighty. I remember what you were like as a mother. You let my piece of shit father beat on me for years, while you drank yourself into oblivion."

Helen sprang from her seat. "What was I supposed to do? I did the best I could."

Lizzie stood from her seat, nodding. "Oh, I understand. When you say that you *did the best you could*, I'm supposed to believe it, but, when I say it, you roll your eyes."

Helen opened her mouth, but nothing came out.

"Why don't you go home, *Mom*. I don't need you anymore."

CHAPTER 39: LUKE AND HOME

Mary and Abby sat before Luke, separated by polycarbonate. His eyes watered at the sight of his family. He hadn't seen Abby in twelve days.

Luke picked up the phone receiver.

Mary did the same, her forehead creased with worry. "What happened to your face?" She referred to the bruising on Luke's jaw.

"It's nothing. I'm fine," Luke replied.

"Did somebody hit you?"

Abby reached toward Luke.

Luke put his hand on the clear partition. "Let me talk to her."

Mary put the phone to Abby's ear.

"Hey, sweet girl," Luke said. "How are you? I've missed you so much."

Abby grinned.

"Look at that smile. So beautiful. Just like your mother. I love you."

Abby turned her head and looked up at her mother.

Mary put the phone back to her ear. "She misses you."

"I miss you both so much," Luke replied, misty-eyed.

"Are you okay? I'm worried about you."

Luke swallowed, his throat tight. "I'm fine. I'm just hoping everything goes well at the preliminary hearing tomorrow."

Mary nodded.

"You'll be there, won't you?"

"Of course."

"I spoke with Gina yesterday. She said if they don't have enough evidence for a trial at the preliminary hearing, they'll have to let me go."

Mary sat up straighter. "Does Gina think that's a possibility?"

"She doesn't think it's likely, but you never know. Think about that. There's a possibility that I'll come home *tomorrow*."

"That's what I'll pray for."

Chapter 40: Curtis and the Barbershop

Curtis sat in the barber's chair, while old Willie buzzed the sides, cleaning up his fade.

"I'm making a video about police abuse of power here in Carville," Curtis said.

"Oh yeah?" Willie replied, checking to make sure Curtis's sideburns were even.

"I was wondering if you wanted to be in it. Maybe you could talk about the time they stole your money."

Willie stepped back and rubbed his chin. "You for real?"

"I'm serious."

"Naw, youngblood. I let that go a long time ago."

"But they're still stealing from people."

"I know. I hear people up in here complaining about the police all the time."

"Don't you want to do something about it?"

"I am doing something about it. I stay the hell away from 'em. Make sure I don't do anything to draw their attention." Willie turned the chair, so Curtis faced the mirror. "Making a video about how they're corrupt is exactly the opposite of that."

After the haircut, Curtis paid Willie and handed him some Justice for Carville business cards. "If you run into anyone who wants to talk, could you give them my card?"

Willie took the business cards. "You got it, youngblood."

With a fresh fade, Curtis walked from the barbershop toward home. As he walked along the rowhomes, he stopped to talk to an elderly woman, sitting on her porch, tapping on her phone. "Excuse me, ma'am?"

The old woman looked up from her phone and scowled. "Do I know you?"

"No, *uh*, I'm with Justice for Carville. My name's Curtis Mays."

"Never heard of it. Or *you* for that matter."

"Justice for Carville is a nonprofit—"

"I ain't got no money."

Curtis flashed his palms. "I'm not looking for donations. I'm working toward police reform. Did you know that the police are excessively ticketing and fining people because the county needs the money?"

"I ain't surprised." The old woman leaned back in her chair. "What's that got to do with me?"

"Well, if you've had any negative experiences with the police, I was hoping you could tell me your story."

"They ain't done shit to me. Unless you count that mess with the code officer."

Curtis stepped closer to the woman. "What mess with the code officer?"

"They sent me a ticket in the mail because my grass was too long. Can you believe that?"

The old woman had a tiny sliver of scalped grass between the sidewalk and her rowhouse.

Curtis pointed at the grass. "For this?"

"You'd think they had better things to do than bother with my grass. It was a little long, but I liked the green. Now I cut it real short, so it don't hardly grow."

"How much did you have to pay?"

She shook her head. "I don't remember exactly, but it was a lot, I remember that. At least two hundred dollars."

"Would you be willing to tell your story for a video I'm working on?"

"You wanna put me on video talking about this? For what?"

"So we can expose the corruption."

The woman laughed. "Child, please. Nobody cares about some ticket I got five years ago."

Curtis thanked the woman for her time and gave her a business card in case she changed her mind. On the way home, he talked to several other Carville residents. They had all been ticketed and fined for minor offenses. One man had been arrested for marijuana possession and had been roughed up during the arrest. But none of the residents were willing to talk about their experiences on camera.

The man who had been arrested had said, "I gotta live here. I don't want no more trouble with the police."

As Curtis neared his house, his cell phone chimed in his pocket. It was Hugh Ellis, the public defender.

"I have great news," Hugh said. "The commonwealth's dropping all the charges against you."

Curtis stopped in his tracks, standing on the sidewalk. "That's great," he replied, with little enthusiasm.

"I thought you'd be more excited."

"Did they say why they're dropping the charges?"

"No, but I assume they didn't think that they had a good case against you."

After Curtis got off the phone, he thought, *What if I had taken the plea deal? How many people get bullied into taking plea deals for shit they didn't do?*

CHAPTER 41: LIZZIE AND THE DEAL

Dennis rolled off Lizzie to his back, his chest rising and falling with his elevated breathing. "*Damn*, Lizzie. You're the best."

She forced a smile but bristled at the casualness of the comment. Lizzie lay on her queen-size bed, naked, her body damp from Dennis's sweat. She checked the clock on her bedside table—*2:04 p.m.* The kids wouldn't be home until three. Thankfully, her mom was long gone.

"You okay?" Dennis asked.

Lizzie snuggled Dennis, placing her head on his chest. "I'm just worried about the preliminary hearing."

He kissed the top of her head. "Well, don't worry. No chance this isn't going to trial."

"I wish he would just take the deal."

"I think he might come around."

Lizzie sat up and turned to Dennis. "Do you know something?"

Dennis grinned.

"*What?*"

Dennis folded the pillow to better prop his head. "Let's just say, we can be *very* persuasive when we're looking after one of our own."

Lizzie's eyes widened in recognition. Then she leaned forward and kissed him on the lips.

CHAPTER 42: LUKE AND THE PRELIMINARY HEARING

Judge Harry Malone sat behind his desk on high. The courtroom clerk sat to the judge's left, behind a shorter desk. The audience crowded into eight rows of wooden pews, separated by a center aisle. Three deputies were strategically positioned around the packed courtroom, not that they were needed. At least half of the audience wore their police uniforms.

Luke sat next to Gina Walters at the defense table. He turned his head, catching a glimpse of Mary and Curtis Mays sitting in the front row of the audience, directly behind the defense table. He faced forward again, not wanting to disobey Gina's instructions, which were to show no emotions and to pay attention to the trial. It didn't play well with the judge if the defendant in a capital murder trial seemed distracted.

Luke glanced at the empty jury box, remembering Gina's explanation. No jury during the preliminary hearing. Gina had mentioned waiving the preliminary hearing altogether, believing that a trial was highly likely, but she thought there was a small chance that the case would be dismissed.

A podium stood between the prosecution and defense tables, facing the judge. The district attorney, Alex Perkins, stood behind the podium. He opened a folder and held up a USB drive inside a plastic bag. A red tab was at the top, identifying the exhibit.

DA Perkins spoke into the mike. "The commonwealth's exhibit number two is the bodycam footage of the altercation on May 7, 2021, between Officer Lambert and the defendant, Luke Archer. Your Honor, this video shows the defendant striking and killing Officer Lambert."

Hushed murmurs came from the audience.

"May I approach the bench?" DA Perkins asked.

Judge Malone motioned for Perkins to bring him the evidence.

DA Perkins delivered the exhibit, then returned to the podium. "The commonwealth calls Officer Larry Dunne to the stand."

One of the deputies led the doughy police officer through the small door in the wooden partition to the witness stand, next to the judge.

After the judge swore him in, DA Perkins asked, "On May 7, 2021, did you receive a dispatch call to Mason's Farm & Feed?"

Officer Dunne leaned into the mike. "I did."

"What was the nature of the call?"

"We received a call that Officer Lambert was unconscious and possibly dead in the parking lot of Mason's Farm & Feed, and the two assailants were still onsite."

"Were you the first officer on the scene?"

"I was."

"What did you see when you arrived?"

"I saw Officer Lambert lying face-first on the macadam, blood pooling around his head. I saw Curtis Mays also on the ground, unconscious. And I saw the defendant, Luke Archer, standing with his back to Officer Lambert, in a daze."

"What do you mean by, *in a daze*?" DA Perkins asked.

Officer Dunne cleared his throat. "His eyes were glazed over. It was like he was a in a trance."

"Was he holding anything in his hand?"

Dunne nodded. "He was holding Officer Lambert's baton."

"Did you notice anything specific about the baton?"

"Yes. It had blood on the end of it."

CHAPTER 43: MARY AND THE BURDEN OF PROBABLE CAUSE

On Friday afternoon, Mary sat in court next to Curtis, just behind Luke and Gina at the defense table.

Judge Harry Malone said, "After reviewing the testimony, as well as exhibits one through seventeen, the court finds that the commonwealth *has* met it's burden of probable cause."

Mary pressed her lips together and clenched her fists, her fingernails digging into her palms.

Luke stared at the tabletop.

The judge continued. "I find that there is probable or sufficient cause to believe that the defendant, Luke Archer, committed first-degree murder of a law enforcement officer, as designated by the criminal complaint."

Curtis whispered to Mary, "Don't worry. This is just the preliminary hearing. Judges rarely throw out any cases."

Chapter 44: Lizzie and Her Best Friend

Emma played in the backyard sandbox, making mounds and holes, letting the sand run between her fingers. Brad had built the box for her and had hauled the fifty-pound bags of sand on his stout shoulders. Brian was at a friend's house, playing video games.

"How are you holding up?" Julie asked, sitting at the patio table with Lizzie, a glass of iced tea before her.

The umbrella shielded the women from the sun.

Lizzie watched Emma, not making eye contact with her best friend. "I'm fine."

"Come on, Lizzie. It's me who you're talking to."

Lizzie turned to Julie. "I really am fine."

Julie stared at her, with raised eyebrows.

"I *am*."

"I texted you on Thursday and Friday. Thought you might want to go to the preliminary hearing together."

"I'm sorry. I guess I've been ... disconnected."

"That's understandable. I'm surprised you didn't go though."

Lizzie looked away. "I just can't deal with it right now."

Julie nodded. "I'm sure you heard, but it went well. The place was filled with police officers. I only saw two people for that piece of shit. His wife and that antipolice activist, Curtis Mays."

"Do you mind if we talk about something else? *Anything* else?" Lizzie took a sip of her iced tea.

"I think Dennis is having an affair."

Lizzie coughed, the iced tea going up her nose. She set the glass back on the table and wiped the iced tea from her nostrils, still coughing.

"Are you okay?" Julie asked.

Lizzie swallowed, her heart thumping in her chest. "What makes you think he's having an affair?"

"He's been more secretive lately. Going into the other room with his phone. I caught him texting someone. He said it was work, but he never needed privacy from me for work stuff before."

"I seriously doubt Dennis would have an affair. He worships you."

Julie huffed. "More like tolerates me."

Lizzie's voice went up an octave. "That's not true."

"Sometimes I smell another woman's perfume on him."

Lizzie thought about the perfume she wore for Dennis, thankful that she rarely wore it anywhere else, especially thankful she wasn't wearing it right then. "Maybe his secretary's wearing new perfume."

Julie huffed again. "Delores? She smells like mothballs and death."

Lizzie pictured Dennis's seventy-year-old secretary. "It could be a witness or a lawyer or even a female cop."

"I really hope you're right, but I don't think so."

"What are you going to do about it?"

Julie took a sip of her iced tea and set the glass back on the table. She stared at Lizzie for a long moment, then said, "I don't know yet."

CHAPTER 45: MARY AND FAITH

"Gina thinks we'll lose," Luke said.

Mary sat across from Luke, the polycarbonate partition between them, plus dividers separating them from the other inmates and their visitors. Abby sat on Mary's lap. "Did Gina actually say that?"

"Not in so many words, but I can tell. It's like she's trying to prepare me for the inevitable."

"But you were protecting Curtis."

Luke shook his head. "It's different with a police officer. Gina said, if the police officer was making a lawful arrest, what I did was ... murder."

Mary frowned. "How can that be a lawful arrest? Curtis was unconscious."

"Even if the arrest was unlawful, a jury has to believe that my actions were in self-defense. I killed a cop. I don't know anyone who'll think that was self-defense." Luke hung his head and rubbed the back of his neck.

"*I* think it was self-defense."

Luke raised his gaze. "I feel like God's forsaken me."

Abby smacked the counter in front of her.

Mary pulled Abby tight to her body, so she couldn't reach the counter. "Don't say that. You have to have faith."

Abby grunted and reached toward Luke.

"I don't know if I can," Luke replied.

Mary quoted a Bible verse. "You must believe and not doubt, because the one who doubts is like a wave of the sea, blown and tossed by the wind."

Luke nodded. "That's exactly what I am now. A wave of the sea, blown and tossed by the wind."

Abby started to cry.

CHAPTER 46: CURTIS AND THE DELIVERY

Curtis hauled small boxes of produce into the Carville Christ Church. Just inside the lobby, a large table was set up, with a sign that read Archer Farms CSA. Customers were already waiting, despite Curtis being early. The designated pickup time was between noon and one. It was only 11:45.

The customers gave Curtis their names and took their boxes of produce. Half of the boxes were collected by noon.

One customer opened her box and asked, "Where's the lettuce?"

Curtis had seen the burned lettuce. "Sorry. We had some problems with the lettuce crop, but we'll have some soon."

For the next hour, Curtis handed out the boxes sporadically, but, as it neared 1:00 p.m., he still had boxes to be collected.

Curtis called Mary. "I still have twelve boxes left," he said. "How long should I wait?"

"Who are they for?" Mary asked.

Curtis read the remaining names from his clipboard.

Mary said, "Fox, Cole, Garretson, and Ebersole canceled this morning. Sorry. I forgot to take them off the list."

"What about the others?"

Mary sighed. "I don't know. Sometimes, instead of canceling, people just stop picking up. Of course, they stop paying too."

Curtis furrowed his brow. "Are they mad about the lettuce?"

"I think they're mad about Luke."

"I'm sorry, Mary."

"It's fine. It'll be *fine*. You have to have faith." Mary said this as if she were trying to convince herself. "Just wait until ten after."

"Okay. See you soon."

Curtis disconnected the call and stared at the twelve remaining names on his list. Examining the entire list, he guessed it was about 20 percent of Mary's customers.

Tisha waltzed into the church, wearing leggings and an oversize T-shirt.

"What are you doing here?" Curtis asked.

"I came to see you," Tisha replied.

Curtis narrowed his eyes. "How did you know I was here?"

"Your dad."

Curtis nodded, his face like stone. "What do you want?"

She glanced at the sign on the table. "You working for Archer Farms now?"

"No. I'm helping them out."

Tisha drew back. "You're not getting paid?"

"No."

She smacked her tongue off the roof of her mouth. "Another black man in chains."

Curtis scowled. "I'm not trying to hear this bullshit. This is my choice. You should check your own chains."

She put her hands on her hips. "Nobody's running me."

"It's easy for you to say. Your parents pay for everything."

"They went to school and got good jobs. I'm not apologizing for that."

"I'm not saying you should."

Tisha crossed her arms over her chest. "What are you saying then?"

"I'm doing the right thing. I don't need your judgment." Curtis checked the time on his phone. "I should go." He scooped up half of the remaining boxes and walked out of the church toward the Archer Farms pickup truck.

Tisha followed. "I'm sorry. I just … I don't want that woman taking advantage of you."

Curtis dropped the tailgate and set the produce in the truck bed. Without making eye contact, he said, "It's my choice to help." Curtis walked back toward the church for the remaining boxes.

Tisha followed. She said to his back, "I heard you were trying to talk to people in Carville about the police."

Curtis stopped and faced Tisha in the parking lot. "What about it?"

"What are you trying to do?"

"Make a documentary about the police corruption."

She nodded. "It's a good idea. Did you have any luck?"

Curtis shook his head.

"You're really bad at asking for help."

Curtis cocked his head. "You offering to help?"

Tisha pursed her full lips. "Do you *want* my help?"

Curtis stepped closer and kissed her.

Chapter 47: Lizzie and the Familiar

Dennis unzipped the blue slacks of his police uniform and fished his erect penis out of the hole of his boxers. He had just arrived at Lizzie's house. Their usual lunchtime tryst. The sex had become rushed and expected.

He pushed down on Lizzie's shoulders, forcing her to her knees. Dennis held Lizzie's head, as she took him in her mouth. He pushed his pelvis forward, causing her to gag. Lizzie tried to pull back, but she was wedged against her bedframe. When he pulled back, removing his penis, she gasped for air.

Dennis reached down and hauled Lizzie to her feet, manipulating her as if she were weightless. His face was beet red. He grasped her shoulders and turned her around, pressing his hand to her upper back, forcing her to bend at the waist.

Dennis yanked her yoga pants and underwear down to midthigh. She sucked in a sharp breath as he entered from behind. She felt a strong sense of déjà vu, as he grunted and thrusted behind her.

Afterward, Lizzie went to her bathroom. She sat on the toilet, wiping semen from her labia and vaginal opening. She dropped the toilet paper in the bowl, flushed, and returned to her bedroom. Dennis tucked his shirt into his slacks, checking himself in her mirror.

Lizzie sat on her made bed and stared at him.

He still fixed his uniform in the mirror.

"Julie thinks you're having an affair," Lizzie announced, as if she were talking about the weather.

Dennis whipped around, glaring at Lizzie. "How the hell do you know that?"

"She came by on Saturday."

Dennis moved closer to Lizzie. "And you're just telling me now?"

Lizzie shrugged. "I never see you on the weekend."

"What did she say?"

"She smelled my perfume on you, and she mentioned you leaving the room to text."

Dennis grimaced. "You need to stop wearing that fucking perfume. Jesus, Lizzie. Why didn't you give me a heads-up?"

"What was I supposed to do? I don't see you on the weekend. Am I supposed to text you, knowing that she's suspicious of that?"

"I assume you told her that she's crazy."

Lizzie clenched her jaw. "I told her that you worship her and that you'd never cheat."

Dennis nodded. "That's good. What did she say?"

Lizzie stood from the bed and held out her hands. "What difference does it make? You don't love her anymore. Why not leave?"

Dennis let out a heavy breath. "It's not that simple. How do you think it would look if I divorced my wife and got together with the wife of a deceased officer? My career would be over. This town is too small for that."

Lizzie crossed her arms over her chest and took a few steps away from Dennis. She stopped in front of the mirror over her dresser and looked at Dennis's reflection. "We shouldn't be sneaking around like this. This is a mistake. We should stop."

Dennis approached from behind, wrapping his arms around her. "Don't say that. It's bad timing but definitely not a mistake. I wish I had met you first."

"Do you?"

"Of course."

Lizzie hung her head. "What's the point if we can't be together without sneaking around?"

"Hey." He turned her to face him, put his hand under her chin, and raised her gaze. "I'm not saying I won't leave Julie. I will, but it's complicated. We have to play this smart, or I could lose my career."

Lizzie nodded.

Dennis kissed her on the cheek. "It's you I wanna be with."

"I think I wanted you before all this. Brad used to accuse me of flirting with you. I think maybe he knew."

"I think I did too," Dennis replied.

Chapter 48: Luke and the Showers

As Luke showered, he noticed the other inmates heading for the locker room. He wondered if his time was up, but usually a guard gave them a countdown. Luke turned off the shower, the room now silent. He grabbed his towel from the short divider wall. As he dried himself, he surveyed the shower area. The other inmates were gone.

His heart pounded, as he walked into the locker room with a towel around his waist. Two fully dressed inmates stood by the exit, with no guards in sight. It was the same two inmates who had beaten Luke in his cell twelve days ago. Luke went to his cubbyhole and grabbed his orange jumpsuit. The two large inmates surrounded him. The tattooed man grinned, purposely showing his upper gums and the tattoo that read Killer.

Luke stared at the man, wondering if he was the devil incarnate. The other inmate, bald and muscly, punched Luke in the stomach.

Luke doubled over, sucking for his lost breath. The tattooed inmate kicked the side of Luke's knee, causing him to topple to the ground, his towel falling from his waist. The inmates stomped and kicked him. Luke covered his head, but the men directed their kicks at his back and stomach. Luke grunted and groaned, as the men pummeled him.

Then, as if on cue, they stopped.

Luke lay on the tile, naked, moaning, and writhing in pain.

The bald inmate stood over Luke, spat in his face, and said, "Take the fuckin' plea."

CHAPTER 49: CURTIS AND ASSET FORFEITURE

Tisha knocked on the front door of the rowhouse. She turned to Curtis and said, "Let me do the talking this time."

"Okay," Curtis replied, holding a case with the camera and tripod.

At the first two houses, Curtis had introduced them and their nonprofit organization. They'd been rejected both times halfway through Curtis's spiel.

An older man opened the door. "Can I help you?"

"Hi. I'm Tisha Hicks. We're part of a nonprofit organization called Justice for Carville. Our mission is to eliminate police abuse in Carville. Did you know that over 40 percent of the Carville budget is met by fines, fees, tickets, and asset forfeiture?"

The man nodded along with Tisha. "That doesn't surprise me one bit."

Tisha gave a sympathetic smile. "You sound like someone who's experienced this firsthand."

The man nodded again. "You could say that."

"I'm sorry to hear that."

The old man narrowed his eyes. "What do you want, young lady? A donation?"

"Donations are appreciated, but that's not why we're here. We're collecting video testimonials from the citizens of Carville, regarding their personal experience with the local police. We're working on a documentary to expose the corruption and abuse our citizens have suffered." Tisha glanced at Curtis, then addressed the old man again. "We'd like to give you a voice."

The man rubbed his stubbly gray beard. "What do I have to do?"

Tisha smiled. "All you have to do is tell your story in your own words for the camera."

"I don't know. I don't need any more problems."

"If we don't speak out, it'll never end."

The old man exhaled. "Hell, I ain't got much left to lose anyway."

The old man invited them inside the cramped house. The lighting was dim; the ceilings were low, and the furniture was brown and mustard colored. Curtis set up the camera and tripod facing the couch in the living room, while Tisha explained the release paperwork.

The old man sat on the couch in front of the camera and asked, "How do I start?"

Curtis stood behind the camera.

"Start with your name and address. Then tell us about your experience with the Carville Police Department," Tisha said. "Just describe what happened to you in your own words."

"Cliff Arnold, 244 Kings Road, Carville, Pennsylvania." The old man cleared his throat. "A few years ago, my youngest son was here. He was out of a job and needed a place to stay, until he got back on his feet. He's a good boy, but he's had some run-ins with the law. Nothin' too serious. Drug possession. He was smokin' marijuana on the back deck, and someone called the police. I didn't know he was doin' that. The police came here, bangin' on the door. You know how they do. Damn near broke the hinges. They said they had probable cause to enter the house because they smelled the marijuana. They must've had special noses 'cause I didn't smell nothin'."

The old man pushed his glasses up his nose. "They trashed my house. Searched every nook and cranny. My house looked like a hurricane blew through it. They found my son's marijuana. Wasn't hardly nothin', but they arrested him. My son was upset, talkin' some mess, and they roughed him up. Not real bad but they had the audacity to charge him with resistin' arrest. Ended up back in prison for six months."

The old man shook his head. "That wasn't all they did neither. I used to keep a little cash on hand, just in case. I've never been one to trust the banks. Anyway, I can tell you this now because I don't keep cash here no more. I used to keep a thousand dollars in some old coffee cans. Those bastards stole that money. Said it was legal. Called it asset forfeiture. Said, because I had drugs in the house, they could assume that cash was from the drug trade. I tried to hire a lawyer, but it would've cost me more than a thousand dollars to get the money back."

CHAPTER 50: LIZZIE AND INSECURITY

Dennis tried to turn Lizzie around, but she resisted.

"Not like that. I want to see you." Lizzie climbed into bed, naked. She lay on her back and motioned with her index finger, a wry smile on her swollen lips.

Dennis positioned himself between her legs and frowned. He masturbated, trying to regain his erection.

"Let me," Lizzie said, reaching for him.

He grunted as she worked her magic, except it didn't work. He was as soft as a marshmallow. Dennis removed her hand from his penis and rolled away from her to his back.

"What's wrong?" Lizzie asked.

"*Nothing*," he snapped. "I'm tired."

Lizzie turned on her side, facing him. "You've never been tired before."

He sat up and exited the bed, a scowl on his face. "I said, I was tired. Leave it alone." He snatched his boxer briefs from the floor.

Lizzie sat up. "You're leaving already?"

Dennis put on his underwear and answered, without making eye contact, "I should get back. I'm meeting with Perkins."

Alex Perkins was the district attorney.

Lizzie drew her knees to her chest. "Is it about the case?"

Dennis put on his shirt and worked the buttons. "He wants background on Brad."

"Why does he need *background*?"

"If they can paint Brad as a violent person, it's favorable to the defense. Perkins wants to know if there are any skeletons he should worry about." Dennis put on his pants.

Lizzie pursed her lips. "Will you tell him about the times I called the station?"

113

Dennis stared at Lizzie for an instant. "Nothing's on file. Don't worry. It's like it never happened."

Lizzie looked down. "But it did happen."

Dennis walked around the bed, shoeless, his shirttail out. He sat on the edge of the bed, next to Lizzie, and turned her gaze to meet his. "None of that matters anymore—"

"Why didn't you stop it?"

Dennis drew back. "*How?* Should I have fired him? Arrested him? Let's say he does six months in prison for domestic abuse. What do you think he's gonna do to you when he gets out? How are you gonna pay the bills while he's in prison?"

"Do you really want to be with me?"

Dennis blew out a breath and stood from the bed. "I don't have time for this."

Lizzie turned away. "You won't leave her, will you?"

He put on his socks and shoes.

Lizzie turned back to Dennis, with tears in her eyes. "You don't give a shit about me, do you?"

"Not when you act like this." Dennis grabbed his keys from the dresser and left.

CHAPTER 51: MARY AND AN UNFAIR TRIAL

Curtis and Tisha were on their hands and knees, cutting asparagus with scissors. Mary did quality control, and bundled the asparagus with rubber bands.

"So ... where did you two meet?" Mary asked.

Curtis dumped a handful of asparagus into the bin. "High school."

Tisha frowned at Curtis. "That's not true. We met at a BLM rally in Philly."

Mary nodded, noncommittal.

Curtis frowned back at Tisha. "We knew *of* each other." Curtis stood and faced Mary. "We ran in similar circles in high school, but Tisha went to Saint Mary's. I went to Carville."

Tisha stood and asked Mary, "What do you think of BLM?"

Mary shrugged. "I don't know much about them."

Tisha narrowed her eyes. "*Really*? Do you think black lives matter? Or do you think all lives matter?"

"Tisha, stop," Curtis said.

"*What*?"

Mary chewed on her bottom lip. "Does it have to be one or the other?"

Curtis addressed Mary. "No. It doesn't."

Tisha raised one side of her mouth in contempt. "It does have to be one or the other."

"For people who are political."

Crying came from the baby monitor in the breast pocket of Mary's overalls. "I'll be back." Mary walked toward her farmhouse.

She heard Curtis say in a hushed voice, "What are you doing?"

Mary went inside, breastfed Abby, then brought her outside in the stroller, with the top up to protect her from the sun. Mary found Curtis and Tisha in the greenhouse at the wash station. Curtis packed the freshly washed asparagus, while Tisha stood nearby.

Mary smiled at her helpers. "Oh, wow. You're already done. Thank you."

"What's next?" Curtis asked.

"That's it," Mary replied. "You two should go do something fun."

"What about the planting?" Curtis gestured to the unplanted rows they had prepped the day before.

"I can do it," Mary replied. "I think Abby's content to sit in her stroller for a while."

Abby started to cry.

Mary lifted Abby from the stroller and bounced her in her arms. Abby cooed, staring at Tisha.

Tisha stepped closer. "She's adorable."

Mary grinned. "Thank you. Would you like to hold her?"

Tisha showed her palms. "Oh, … that's okay."

"Here." Mary handed Abby to Tisha.

Tisha took the handoff like Abby was a priceless crystal. Tisha cradled Abby, making googly eyes at the baby. Abby smiled.

"She likes you," Mary said.

Tisha rocked Abby in her arms, as Mary had done.

"You're a natural."

Tisha beamed, her gaze locked on Abby. Curtis watched Tisha's motherly instinct in action. Mary wondered if Curtis wanted children with Tisha.

Tisha handed Abby back to Mary. "She's so sweet."

"Most of the time," Mary replied.

"I'm sorry about giving you a hard time earlier. All that BLM stuff."

"It's okay."

"It's just …" Tisha glanced at Curtis. "Curtis is working here a lot …"

"I'm here because I want to be here," Curtis interjected.

"I understand," Mary said, glancing at Curtis. "I know I'm taking advantage."

"You're not," Curtis said, interjecting again.

Tisha pursed her lips. "I don't think this is you, but I've been around a lot of white people who say they care about black people, but, when it comes down to making a real sacrifice, they're all talk."

"The white people you're talking about are virtue-signaling college kids," Curtis said to Tisha. "Mary never said anything about black people, and Luke made the ultimate sacrifice for me. Not black people. *Me.*"

"I have to be honest," Mary said. "I know nothing about black people. You two are the only black people I've met in my whole life."

"*Really?*" Tisha asked.

"I grew up Amish. Everybody in my community was white and German. We didn't interact with the English that much. Even now, most of my life is on the farm."

"I'm just wondering how long this will go on?" Tisha asked.

Curtis gave her a look. "*Tisha.*"

Tisha looked from Curtis to Mary. "Seriously. What happens if Luke's convicted? It's a legit concern."

Mary lifted one shoulder. "I don't ..."

Tisha turned to Curtis. "Are you prepared to work here for free for twenty years?"

"That won't happen," Curtis said.

"I would never expect ..." Mary said, clutching Abby tight to her chest.

"How do you know?" Tisha replied to Curtis, ignoring Mary's comment. "You know how the system works. Luke has a public defender. He won't get a fair trial. It helps that he's white, but he doesn't have money."

Mary felt sick to her stomach.

"Mary doesn't need to hear this," Curtis said to Tisha. "She has enough to deal with."

"I think I *do* need to hear this," Mary said.

Curtis opened his mouth to speak, but nothing came out.

"I think we need to look closer at the case," Tisha said to Mary. "Maybe go to the feedstore and look around. Curtis might remember something that could help."

CHAPTER 52: CURTIS AND THE SCENE OF THE CRIME

Tisha parked her Honda Civic in the parking lot of Mason's Farm & Feed, along the right side of the building. They exited the car. Curtis scanned the mostly empty parking lot. A wave of déjà vu passed over him. Officer Lambert's red face. Lambert pounding on Curtis's back with the baton. Trying in vain to contort his body away from the beating.

Tisha touched his forearm. "Are you okay?"

Curtis blinked back to reality. "I'm fine. Let's look around."

They walked around the parking lot to the right of the building. The front had a few parking spaces too, but that's not where the altercation had occurred. Curtis told the story to Tisha again, showing her where the man in the Toyota Corolla had been pulled over and where Curtis had filmed the traffic stop. Then he showed her where Officer Lambert had parked his cruiser and where they had had the verbal altercation that turned violent.

Curtis pointed to a spot on the macadam. "This is about where he stepped on my phone."

"Maybe we can find pieces of it," Tisha replied. "That could prove Lambert was trying to hide what he was doing."

"I bet they cleaned it up, but we might as well look."

They searched the spot, expanding out in a circle.

"There's nothing," Curtis said.

Tisha turned from the macadam to Curtis, the side of Mason's Farm & Feed in the background. Something caught her eye on the feedstore wall. She pointed at the top of it. "Look at that."

Curtis turned to look at the feedstore. "What?"

Tisha walked closer to the building, pointing to the upper corner of the wall. "Up there. See that clean circle?"

The north-facing wall had a thin layer of mold on the tan siding, but, at the top, there was a clean circle about the size of a large hamburger, with a small hole in the middle.

"I see it," Curtis said, fast-walking to the front of the building. He spotted a camera aimed at the front parking lot. The circular base of the camera was the identical size of the clean circle on the right side of the building.

"A camera was there," Tisha said.

Curtis turned to Tisha and replied, "This can't be a coincidence."

They circled the building, finding another camera on the left side and another in back.

As they walked back to Tisha's car, Curtis said, "I bet the cops took the camera."

"Why would they do that?" Tisha asked. "They already have the bodycam footage."

"I don't know. Maybe it shows something that the bodycam doesn't."

They stopped in front of Tisha's Honda.

"Like what?" Tisha asked.

"In the preliminary hearing, when they were showing the *confession*"—Curtis threw up air quotes when he said *confession*—"Luke said that Lambert pulled his gun, but you couldn't see that on the bodycam footage."

"Even if that's true, the cops can point their guns at people. Shit, they do it all the time."

"That may be, but the more it looks like Lambert was trying to kill Luke, the more likely a jury will acquit."

Tisha nodded. "That's a good point."

"And, if the cops did take the camera, then they're tampering with evidence, and that would also be a huge win for Luke."

"Even if the cops did take the camera, it's not like they'll tell us."

"Maybe somebody else knows." Curtis gestured to the feedstore.

Tisha grinned. "Let me do the talking."

They went inside Mason's Farm & Feed. They approached the old man at the counter. The man's face was sunspotted, and his white hair was disheveled.

"Can I help you?" the old man asked.

Tisha smiled. "I hope so. My name's Tisha." She gestured to Curtis. "This is my colleague, Curtis."

Curtis smiled wide, hoping to put the old man at ease.

The old man narrowed his eyes at Curtis, as if trying to place him, but Curtis had never met the man.

Curtis wondered if the man had seen him on the missing security camera. *Or maybe he saw me on the news.*

Tisha continued. "We run a nonprofit called Justice for Carville. We're helping Luke Archer with his defense."

The old man stiffened.

Tisha continued. "Are you the owner of this store?"

The old man nodded. "I am."

"May I ask your name?" Tisha asked.

"Fred Mason."

Tisha smiled again. "It's so nice to meet you, Mr. Mason."

Mr. Mason grunted. "What's your name, young lady?"

Curtis and Tisha glanced at each other, knowing that she had just introduced them.

Tisha reintroduced herself and Curtis.

Mr. Mason grunted again. "What can I do for you?"

"Well, we were wondering if you had the camera footage from Luke's ... accident," Tisha asked.

Mr. Mason appeared confused. "What accident?"

Curtis interjected. "The accident in your parking lot, where Officer Lambert was killed."

Mr. Mason's face was blank for a few seconds, then it registered, and he shook his head. "Nope. Sorry. That camera doesn't work."

"There's no camera on that side of the building," Curtis said. "Did something happen to it?"

Mr. Mason broke eye contact for a beat. "It's broken. Don't know what happened to it."

"When did you take it down?"

Mr. Mason paused for a moment. "Couple years ago."

Curtis drew his eyebrows together. "There's a clean circle on your building where the camera used to be. It looks like the camera was taken down recently."

"Don't know nothin' about that."

Curtis stepped closer, staring at Mr. Mason, only separated by the counter. "Did the police take the camera?"

Mr. Mason frowned. "I already told you. I threw it away last year."

"You said two years ago."

"I think it's best you folks left."

Tisha said, "If you're being threatened by the police—"

"Go on. *Git.*" Mr. Mason pointed at the door.

Tisha put her hands on her hips, her stance wide, as if daring Mr. Mason to make her leave.

Curtis grabbed Tisha by the elbow, not wanting her to argue with the old man. "Come on."

They left the feedstore and climbed into Tisha's Honda.

"The cops took that camera," Tisha said.

"I know, but he won't talk to us," Curtis replied.

Tisha put on her seat belt and started the car. "We're not the right people to persuade that old white man to talk."

Curtis put on his seat belt too. "Who are the right people?"

"How about a pretty white woman in distress?" Tisha turned to Curtis, with arched eyebrows. "You know any?"

CHAPTER 53: LIZZIE AND "LUNCH" WITH DENNIS

Lizzie inspected herself in the mirror. Her baby-doll negligee was nearly clear and hung just below her crotch. She wore lacy thong underwear and no bra. She put her hands on her hips. *This'll get his motor running.*

A knock came at the side door. Dennis and Lizzie had been meeting most weekdays during his lunch hour. Lizzie slipped on her white high heels. As she strutted down the hall to the kitchen, she thought she should give Dennis a house key. She opened the door, a wry smile on her lips.

Julie gaped at Lizzie, her eyes wide.

Lizzie sucked in a sharp breath. Her voice was higher than usual. "Julie. What are you doing here?"

Julie raised one side of her mouth in contempt. "Am I interrupting something?"

"No, I, uh, … I was just trying some stuff on. I saw it was you, otherwise I wouldn't have opened the door." She waved Julie inside and giggled. "Come in before the neighbors see me."

Julie stepped inside, peering at Lizzie through narrowed eyes.

Lizzie shut the door behind her. "I'll be right back. I should change—"

"Let's not do this," Julie said. "I know you've been sleeping with Dennis, and you were obviously expecting him."

"It's not like that. I swear."

Julie held up her hand. "*Stop.* You're embarrassing yourself."

Lizzie hugged herself, trying to cover up.

"I'm not here to debate with you. I'm here to tell you that it's over. Dennis will no longer see you, under any circumstances." Julie stepped uncomfortably close to Lizzie. "If you try to contact him again, we'll file stalking charges." Julie put her finger in Lizzie's face. "Don't *fucking* test me." Julie pivoted and marched to the side door. She opened the door and turned back to Lizzie one last time. "He never loved you. You were nothing but a white-trash side piece." Julie slammed the door and left.

Lizzie kicked off her high heels, ran to her bedroom, and grabbed her cell phone from her dresser top. She called Dennis. After a single ring, her call went to voice mail. She sent him a frantic text.

Lizzie: She knows. She said it's over between us. CALL ME!!!!!

Lizzie stared at her text messages, hoping for a response.

CHAPTER 54: MARY AND BLESSED ARE THE PEACEMAKERS

Luke moved with the speed of an octogenarian, wincing as he sat before Mary, on the other side of the polycarbonate divider.

Mary watched him struggle, her stomach in knots. She'd left Abby with a neighbor, as she was too crabby for a jail visit. Mary put her phone receiver to her ear.

Luke put his phone receiver to his ear.

"What's wrong?" Mary asked, leaning toward the clear partition.

His face appeared unharmed, but he was obviously in pain.

"It's nothing," Luke replied.

"What do you mean, *it's nothing*? You can barely walk."

"I'll be fine."

"What happened?"

Luke looked around, then whispered, "They want me to take the plea."

Mary furrowed her brow. "What does that have to do with anything?"

"I think powerful people are doing this to me."

"Doing what?"

"Other inmates." Luke swallowed hard. "They attacked me. When it was over, they told me to take the plea."

Mary's voice went up an octave. "They can't do that. We have to tell someone about this."

Luke looked around again and spoke in a harsh whisper. "*Who*? The police? The prison guards? They let it happen."

Tears filled Mary's eyes. "They can't do this. I'll talk to Gina. Maybe she can help."

"Please, don't. You'll make it worse for me. *They* have the power."

"That's what worries me."

"Don't worry. God will protect me."

Mary shook her head, tears slipping down her face. "This isn't about God. You have to defend yourself."

Luke placed his large hand on the polycarbonate. "Blessed are the peacemakers, for they will be called sons of God."

Mary placed her tiny hand on the polycarbonate, mirroring her husband's. "Please defend yourself. I *need* you to come home."

CHAPTER 55: CURTIS AND THE WITNESS

Curtis held the door to the feedstore for Mary and Abby.

Mr. Mason mean-mugged Curtis and Mary, marching toward the counter. Before they could speak, Mr. Mason said, "I got nothin' else to say."

Curtis gestured to Mary, holding Abby in her arms. "This is who you're hurting. She's a real person with a baby."

Mary held up her hand to Curtis, like a stop sign. "It's okay." Then she addressed Mr. Mason, her voice soothing. "Luke and I are really struggling. Please, Mr. Mason. We need your help. If you know *anything* ..."

Mr. Mason slumped his shoulders. "I can't help you."

Mary stiffened. "Can't or won't?"

"What's the difference?"

Curtis interjected. "The cops took the video, didn't they?"

The front door opened, and a customer entered the store.

Mr. Mason said, "Leave me alone. I don't know nothin'." The customer stood a few feet behind Curtis and Mary. Mr. Mason looked around them, waved the customer forward, and said, "Can I help you?"

Curtis glared at Mr. Mason. "We're not done."

The customer stepped back.

Mr. Mason glared back at Curtis. "You *are* done."

"We're not leaving," Mary said.

"Don't make me call the police."

Curtis crossed his arms over his chest. "You want them to beat me unconscious again?"

The customer left the store.

Mr. Mason broke eye contact. His voice was barely audible, almost childlike. "Please leave me alone."

"Please, Mr. Mason. We need your help," Mary said.

Mr. Mason hung his head. "I can't. Please leave."

"Luke's facing life in prison."

Mr. Mason picked up the handset from his desktop phone and dialed 9-1-1. He listened for a few seconds, then said, "Two people are in my store, and they're refusing to leave."

Mary touched Curtis's elbow. "Let's go."

They left the feedstore.

In the parking lot, Curtis said, "He's hiding something."

Mary adjusted Abby in her arms. "It doesn't matter, if he won't talk to us."

CHAPTER 56: LIZZIE AND UNREQUITED

Over the Memorial Day weekend, Lizzie had sent over one hundred texts and left dozens of messages for Dennis, each message more urgent than the last, culminating in a profanity-laced tirade.

Now, on Tuesday morning, she marched into the Carville police station.

A young uniformed officer sat at the front desk. Nobody Lizzie knew. Probably just out of the police academy.

"Can I help you?" the officer asked.

"I need to talk to Chief Rhodes," Lizzie said, peering beyond the front desk, hoping to catch a glimpse of Dennis.

"Do you have an appointment?"

"No."

"I can see if he's in, but you'll probably have to make an appointment."

"He'll see me."

The officer checked Lizzie's ID, then called Dennis's office. He hung up the phone and said, "I'm sorry. Chief Rhodes is busy. Would you like to schedule an appointment?"

Lizzie glowered at the young officer. "Call him back and tell him that he'll regret it if he doesn't talk to me."

The officer stood from his seat, his face like stone. "Was that a threat, ma'am?"

"My husband was Brad Lambert."

The officer checked her name on his log sheet. "I, I'm sorry. I didn't know."

"Call Chief Rhodes back and tell him that it's an emergency, and I'm not leaving without talking to him."

He nodded and called Dennis again, relaying Lizzie's message. The officer hung up the phone again and said, "I'll take you back."

Lizzie followed the young officer to Dennis's open office door.

Dennis met them at the doorway. "Thanks, Connors."

The young officer left.

Dennis shut the door behind them.

Lizzie had her hands on her hips. "Did you have a nice weekend?"

Dennis grabbed her by the elbow and led her away from the door to the couch, but they didn't sit. "What the *hell* do you think you're doing?" He spoke in a hushed whisper, his finger jabbing the space between them.

Lizzie held out her hands. "What am I supposed to do? You're ignoring me."

"I'm gonna tell you this *once*. It's *over*. You come here again, and I'll arrest you myself."

Lizzie huffed. "For what?"

"I'll fucking find something."

Lizzie slapped him across the face.

Dennis touched his cheek. "Assaulting a police officer oughta do."

Tears filled Lizzie's eyes. "Why are you doing this? I thought you wanted to be with me."

Dennis raised one side of his mouth in contempt.

"Please don't do this." She tried to hug him.

Dennis pushed her away, holding her at arm's length. "Get yourself together and go home."

Tears slipped down Lizzie's cheeks. "Please, Dennis. I don't care if it has to be a secret. I can't lose you too."

"It's *over*. Go home, Lizzie."

Lizzie sniffled, wiped her face with her T-shirt, and said, "You took advantage of me. Pretending to be there for me, when all you really wanted was sex." She huffed. "I thought we had a future."

"You're delusional. I'm done with you." He pointed to the door. "Get the fuck out, and don't come back."

She stared at Dennis for a long moment. "I'll tell the whole town how you took advantage of a grieving widow."

Dennis grabbed her by the neck, with both hands, squeezing like a python.

Lizzie choked, her eyes bulging, her face beet red.

He spoke through gritted teeth. "You think you can threaten me?"

Lizzie pawed at his forearms to no avail. Her vision blurred without oxygen. She was overcome with a strong sense of déjà vu.

Dennis let go, giving her a little shove for good measure.

Lizzie stumbled backward, sucking in oxygen. She wheezed and bent over, her hands on her knees.

Dennis stood over her. "If you say anything, I'll make your life a living hell."

Lizzie stood upright, took a deep breath, and said, "You'll regret this."

His lips curled into a sneer. "I already do."

She left his office, slamming the door in her wake.

CHAPTER 57: LUKE AND TOO FAR

Luke lay on the bottom bunk, the bed barely able to contain his length. The lights flicked off, only the safety lights providing ambient light. He thought about the empty bunk above him, wondering why he still didn't have a new cellmate. He wasn't sure if he wanted one. He imagined Mary's beautiful face. A pang of guilt churned deep in the pit of his stomach for failing to take care of his family.

His door unlocked with a *clunk*.

Luke tensed but didn't move. He caught a glimpse of the guard holding the door, followed by two inmates entering his cell, the same inmates who had beaten him twice before. The bald inmate grabbed Luke by the ankles and pulled him from the bottom bunk, depositing Luke onto the concrete floor. Luke curled into the fetal position, covering his head.

"What a pussy," the tattooed inmate said.

The bald inmate bent down close to Luke's face, exhaling his foul breath. "Take the fuckin' plea deal."

Tears welled in Luke's eyes. He spoke without making eye contact, his voice quivering, still with his head covered by his arms. "I can't. I'll never see my family again."

The tattooed inmate cackled. "This motherfucker's cryin'."

The bald inmate inched closer and whispered, "Mary. That's your wife, right?"

Luke clenched his fists, adrenaline coursing through his veins.

"I know a guy who'll go to your house and fuck your little wife."

With the speed of a viper, Luke turned over and grabbed the man by the back of his head. The bald inmate was bent down, cramped, and in an awkward position. Luke pulled him down headfirst. The bald inmate's face smacked the concrete, breaking his nose, blood splattering

131

on the floor. Luke crawled on top of his back, still in control of the man's head. Luke smashed the bald inmate's face into the concrete again, the large man going out like a light. The tattooed inmate jumped on Luke's back, trying to put him in a chokehold.

Luke screamed at the top of his lungs, rose to his feet, the inmate still on his back. Luke backpedaled, ramming the tattooed inmate against the prison wall. The inmate groaned with the impact but still held on. Luke reached behind his head, grabbing the man by the neck. He bent down and whipped the tattooed man forward, tossing him to the ground, the bald man breaking his fall. The tattooed inmate scrambled to his feet and ran from the cell.

The bald inmate lay motionless on the floor, blood spilling from his head. Luke was overcome with a sense of déjà vu. But, this time, the man groaned and crawled for the exit.

Two beefy prison guards entered Luke's cell with their billy clubs in hand, the same two prison guards who had previously "encouraged" him to take the plea deal. Luke raised his hands over his head.

The mustachioed guard jabbed Luke in the stomach with the end of his billy club. Luke went down, gasping for air. The guards beat Luke's back and midsection with their billy clubs. Luke curled into a fetal position, taking his beating without complaint, until the two guards were out of breath.

Then the mustachioed guard said, "You're goin' to seg."

Chapter 58: Curtis and Technical Support

Several streetlights were out. The remaining bulbs cast blobs of light too far apart to adequately illuminate the neighborhood. Curtis rode his bike on a cracked sidewalk in Carville, passing dilapidated rowhouses. He slowed his bike, as he approached the silhouette of a man and a woman. They were in front of a condemned rowhouse, doing a hand-to-hand exchange, just outside the glow of the streetlights.

Curtis stopped his bike, thinking about turning around.

"Get the fuck outta here," the man said to the woman.

The woman scurried away, her hand gripped around a plastic baggie.

Curtis recognized Daryl's voice. He dismounted and walked up to Daryl, pushing his bike.

Daryl lifted his chin. "What's up?"

"What was that?" Curtis asked, gesturing to the fleeing woman.

"You need somethin'?"

"I texted you."

"I got shit goin' on. What you need?"

Curtis looked around, making sure they were alone. "I'm trying to get into Mason's Farm & Feed."

Daryl raised his eyebrows. "You tryin' to rob the place?"

Curtis frowned. "It's not like that. I need some video footage."

"Luke Archer."

Curtis nodded. "I think there's video that could help his case."

"If you steal it, they can't use that shit in court."

"I know. I think it could help with public opinion, and public opinion can sway a jury."

Daryl slipped his hands into the front pocket of his hoodie. "What you need me for?"

"Technical support."

Daryl chuckled. "Yeah. I could do that."

"I just need you to tell me how to do it."

Daryl shook his head. "Naw, I'll show you."

Chapter 59: Lizzie and the Public Defender

"Have a seat," Gina Walters said, gesturing to the plastic chair in front of her desk.

Lizzie sat, facing Luke Archer's defense attorney.

The office was a tiny box, cluttered with filing cabinets.

Gina sat rigid in her leather swivel chair. "This is quite a surprise."

Lizzie nodded.

"Does the DA know you're here?"

"No."

"What can I do for you?"

Lizzie hesitated. "Was my husband ... ever accused of police brutality? I mean, before all this happened."

Gina narrowed her eyes. "Not that I know of. I requested your husband's personnel file, for precisely this reason, but I was denied access. The state has the legal right to refuse to disclose personnel data, if there is no reason to think it would be helpful or relevant to the defense's case. Is there evidence that I should be aware of?"

Lizzie stood from her seat. "I'm sorry. This was a mistake." She hurried from the office.

Gina called out to her back, "Mrs. Lambert."

CHAPTER 60: CURTIS AND THE MONEY

Curtis and Daryl crept up to the right side of Mason's Farm & Feed, both wearing dark clothing and ski masks. The parking lot was empty and dimly lit. A vehicle drove by every thirty seconds or so, but it was doubtful that they were spotted in the darkness.

"There's no camera here," Curtis said, his back to the wall.

Daryl peered into the window.

Curtis turned around and did the same. The feedstore was dark inside, except for the exit signs and the dim ambient light from the parking lot.

Daryl removed his backpack, opened it, and retrieved a crowbar.

"What are you doing?" Curtis asked in a hushed whisper.

"Bustin' this window."

"What about the alarm?"

Daryl pointed to the sash on the double-hung window. "There'd be a contact on the window frame. Ain't no contact, ain't no alarm on the window. Could be a motion sensor inside though."

"What do we do if there's a motion sensor?"

Daryl chuckled. "Run." He jabbed the window with his crowbar, smashing the glass.

Curtis looked around, worried that they were being too loud.

Daryl smashed all the glass squares on the lower half of the window, seemingly unconcerned by the noise. Then, using wire cutters, he cut and removed the plastic grid. He turned to Curtis and said, "Let's get it."

Daryl went through the window headfirst. Curtis braced himself for the alarm, but it was quiet, except for the breeze and the occasional car driving past. Curtis climbed through the window, breaking his fall with his gloved hands. Curtis stood and grabbed his flashlight from his pocket.

"Hurry up," Daryl said. "Could be a silent alarm."

Curtis rushed toward the front counter, his flashlight illuminating the space. Behind the counter was a shut door. Curtis tried to turn the knob. "It's locked."

"Move over," Daryl said, nudging Curtis aside. Daryl kicked the flimsy door, busting the lock.

Daryl and Curtis entered the office. Inside was a laminate desk, computer, and metal filing cabinets. Curtis went to the computer, turned on the laptop, and sat at the desk. Pictures of Fred Mason with his family were on the desk. Daryl opened the filing cabinets, checking the drawers. As the computer loaded, Curtis opened the top drawer, searching for a USB drive but only finding office supplies. As he shut the drawer, he noticed a black box under the desk.

Curtis shone his flashlight at the box. "I found a safe."

Daryl appeared at Curtis's side. "Let's move the desk."

Curtis unplugged the laptop and the printer. Then they grabbed each end of the desk and moved it toward the door, away from the safe. Daryl cranked on the little safe with his crowbar. Curtis rolled the chair to the desk and went back to the laptop. After a few minutes, he found the security camera footage. He searched the database for May 7, 2021, the day of Curtis and Luke's arrests. He found footage for cameras one, two, three, and four. Camera two was the missing camera. It covered the right-hand parking lot, where the altercation had occurred. *The old man was lying. That camera was working.*

He played the video in question, forwarding until he saw Officer Lambert's cruiser and the Toyota Corolla in the parking lot. Shortly thereafter, Luke Archer's truck arrived. Curtis grinned. *Got it.* Curtis watched Luke park alongside the feedstore and exit his truck. As Luke entered the feedstore, Curtis arrived on the scene, riding his bike. Then Curtis disappeared, along with the Toyota Corolla, and Officer Lambert. *What the hell?* Police officers secured the scene, putting up police tape around the parking area. Curtis rewound a few seconds and played the video again, this time watching the time stamp. After a few seconds, the video jumped forward again, and the time stamp skipped forward by an hour.

"Shit," Curtis said.

"What is it?" Daryl asked, still working on the safe.

"I think the cops erased the video. Let me know when you get that open. Maybe old man Mason put a copy in the safe." Curtis didn't think it was likely.

"I got you."

Curtis forwarded the video, watching the police move around the scene with cartoonlike rapidity, then the video went black. He searched the database for camera two footage on May 8, 2021, but there was nothing beyond what he saw. *The cops must've made Fred Mason delete the footage, then they took the camera too.*

"Got it," Daryl said, the safe now open, the locking mechanism mangled and bent by the crowbar.

Curtis turned around in the swivel chair. "Is there a USB drive in there?"

"Just this." Daryl opened a blue deposit bag and grinned. "Cash money."

Curtis stood from the swivel chair. "We're not here for that."

"This ain't for you."

Curtis stepped closer to his friend. "Come on, Daryl. Put it back."

Daryl held up his finger to Curtis. He cocked his head, listening. Curtis heard a faint siren.

"Let's go." Daryl ran from the office, still holding the deposit bag.

Curtis checked the open safe, confirming that it was empty, then ran after his friend. They climbed out of the broken window. The siren was much louder outside. Lights flashed in the distance. Daryl ran for the woods and the creek that ran behind the feedstore. Curtis chased him, adrenaline coursing through his veins. This was the preplanned escape route, but it was darker than Curtis had anticipated, and he was too afraid to use his flashlight. He tripped on a tree root and fell forward, banging his knees and palms on the forest floor.

Curtis scrambled to his feet and hustled down the embankment to the shallow creek. He played leapfrog, stepping from large rock to large rock, trying to avoid the creek water. Once on the other side, Curtis ran up hill, until he reached an abandoned gas station. He took off his ski mask, before he emerged from the forest.

Daryl stood next to his vintage Chevy Impala SS, a big smile on his face.

Curtis scowled as he approached his friend. "Give me the money. I'll send it back."

Daryl sneered. "I ain't givin' you shit. This is my fuckin' money."

Curtis clenched his jaw. "I told you that I only wanted the video."

"That's your business. The money's my business."

Curtis spotted the deposit bag in the front seat of Daryl's car. Curtis stepped around Daryl and reached through his open window.

Daryl grabbed Curtis and shoved him to the ground. "What the fuck you think you're doin'?"

Curtis rose to his feet, staring at Daryl. "Give me the money."

"What you goin' do, nigga?"

Curtis walked toward the car, reaching into the window again. This time Daryl grabbed Curtis by the collar and threw a right cross, connecting with Curtis's jaw. Curtis's legs wobbled, and he fell to one knee. Daryl swung again, this punch connecting with Curtis's chin and sending him to his side, the world spinning above him.

Daryl stood over Curtis and said, "Stay down, motherfucker."

Daryl got into his car and chirped the tires, as he sped away from the old gas station.

Chapter 61: Luke and Suffering for God

Luke lay on his back, taking shallow breaths, each inhalation and exhalation causing a stabbing pain in his ribcage. The single bunk in seg—segregation—had only a thin stained mattress separating him from the metal. He put his hand in front of his face, but it was too dark to see it.

Luke imagined an alternate reality, one where he'd never killed a man. He pictured himself a few years into the future, teaching Abby to ride a bicycle, holding the seat as she steadied herself, and running after her to make sure she didn't fall. Mary cheered them on, holding a little boy in her arms.

He spoke in a whisper, mindful of his injuries. "I give you my body, my suffering, and my soul. Please, God, I only ask that You protect Mary and Abby." He thought of a Bible verse, speaking louder, and feeling the pain in his ribs. "Therefore, since Christ suffered in his body, arm yourselves also with the same attitude, because whoever suffers in the body is done with sin."

He repeated the Bible verse, even louder this time, searing pain coming from his midsection. Then again and again, like a mantra, until he shouted the verse, the suffering bringing him closer to God.

CHAPTER 62: MARY AND PROOF

Morning dew still covered the plants. Mary cut bundles of rainbow-colored chard, tied them together with a rubber band, and set them in her crate. The roar of a pickup truck caused her to look up from her work. Curtis drove his dad's truck.

Mary smiled. She had told Curtis that she didn't need his help that Friday, but she was grateful nonetheless. She went to meet him. Curtis parked his truck behind Mary's. They met in front of the farmhouse.

Her smile evaporated when she saw the bruising on his face. "What happened to you?"

Curtis touched his chin. "I got into a fight with my friend, Daryl, but that's not important."

Mary narrowed her eyes, inspecting his face. "Are you okay?"

"I'm fine. Look. I know that the police took the video from Fred Mason."

"We figured as much, but nobody's talking."

"I have definitive proof. There's footage for the missing camera on May seventh, and then, right after Luke showed up at the feedstore, it's cut off for about an hour. Then you see the cops putting up police tape. I think the cops made Fred Mason erase the footage. The cops must be threatening him or something. We need to talk to him again."

Mary tilted her head. "Mr. Mason didn't show you this?"

"No."

"I don't understand. How did you find this out?"

Curtis took a deep breath. "I broke into the feedstore and got on his computer."

Mary twisted her face in disgust. "*Curtis*. Why would you do that?"

"Because he's lying. Luke's life is on the line."

Mary glared at Curtis. "You think I don't know that?"

Curtis showed his palms. "I know you know. I'm just saying that breaking and entering's nothing compared to Luke's life—"

"How does this even help? You can't testify that you broke into the feedstore."

"We can confront Mr. Mason again. Get *him* to testify."

"You think breaking into his store will get him to testify? I'm assuming you damaged his store to get in."

"We broke a window … and a safe, but that's it."

Mary drew back. "Wait a second. Who's we?"

Curtis winced and said, "My friend, Daryl."

"The same one who punched you in the face?"

Curtis nodded.

"Did you steal anything?"

Curtis's voice went up an octave. "Of course not. I would never do that."

Mary stared at Curtis for a long moment. "What about Daryl?"

"He took some money, but I'll get it back. I promise. We need to go talk to Mr. Mason. He could be the key to freeing Luke."

Mary shook her head, her face like stone. "You need to leave. Until you return that money, I don't want you here."

"Mary, please."

Mary pointed to his truck. "Leave. *Now.*"

CHAPTER 63: CURTIS AND NO GOOD DEED

Late on Friday afternoon, Curtis rode his bike to Daryl's house, the warm sun on his face. The brick rowhouse was technically Daryl's mother's house. Curtis knocked on the door.

Daryl's mother, Denise Porter, answered the door with a wide smile. "Curtis. What a pleasant surprise. I haven't seen you in a minute."

Curtis smiled back at the tall woman, who probably could've been a model, had she not dedicated her life to third-graders. "It's nice to see you, Mrs. Porter." Curtis always called her Mrs. Porter, even though she'd never married. When they were young Curtis and Daryl had tried to get Denise together with Leonard, thinking that it would be cool if they were brothers. Daryl told his mother that Curtis's dad liked her, and Curtis told his dad that Daryl's mom liked him. Both kids then encouraged their parent to ask the other parent out on a date. Their Cupid attempt didn't work, but the parents had a good laugh.

"Daryl's not here right now," Denise said.

"He's supposed to meet me here. He's helping me with some Justice for Carville stuff. You know, the nonprofit that Tisha and I started?" Curtis checked the time on his phone. "I'm a little early."

"I think it's so wonderful that you two are trying to make a difference. I wish Daryl would spend more time with you."

Curtis nodded. "Me too."

"You can come in and wait, if you want."

"Thank you."

Curtis followed Denise to the kitchen. "You want something to drink? I just made sweet tea."

"Sure. Thank you, Mrs. Porter."

Denise poured Curtis a glass of tea.

They sat at the kitchen table.

"I'm glad you're here," Denise said. "I've been meaning to talk to you."

Curtis swallowed some tea and set the glass before him.

"I've been worried about you. All this mess with that officer dying and all. Are you okay?"

Curtis nodded again. "I'm fine. Thank you."

Denise arched her eyebrows. "You sure about that? What happened to your face?"

Curtis touched his face. "It's nothing. I was playing basketball. Caught an elbow to the face."

Denise winced. "Must've hurt."

Curtis forced a smile. "A little bit."

"Well, I'm glad you're doing okay. If you need anything, you can always come here."

"Thank you." Curtis gulped his tea, the cold drink refreshing after his bike ride.

Denise took a deep breath. "I also wanted to ask you about Daryl. He's been acting a fool lately. Coming home at all hours of the night, like my house is a hotel. Copping an attitude whenever I ask him what he's been doing. The boy isn't working, yet he somehow bought a car. New clothes and shoes. Expensive jewelry." Denise sighed. "Is he dealing drugs?"

Curtis swallowed. "I ... I'm not sure, Mrs. Porter."

Denise leaned toward Curtis, her elbows on the table. "I need your help. I don't know what to do. I see my son going down the wrong path, but I can't do anything about it. He barely says two words to me."

"I'll try to talk to him, if you want?"

Denise reached out and touched Curtis's hand. "I knew I could count on you." She removed her hand and let out a cleansing breath. "You've always been a good friend."

Curtis swallowed hard.

Denise stood from the table. "I have some work to do, but you're welcome to watch TV while you wait."

"Is it okay if I wait in Daryl's room?"

"Go right ahead." She smirked. "I'll give you twenty dollars if you clean it."

Denise went to her home office, while Curtis went upstairs to Daryl's room. Curtis shut the door behind him. A vintage stereo stood in the corner with a turntable. A clothes pile was in another corner. The single bed was unmade. Rap stars and scantily clad young women adorned the walls. A few dirty plates sat on his dresser top. A few more on his desk.

Curtis rifled through his drawers, searching for the cash, but found nothing out of the ordinary—except for Daryl's stash of weed. He went to the desk, checking all the drawers, but again found nothing. Curtis opened Daryl's closet. It was the neatest part of the room, with the Air Jordan sneaker collection displayed on tilted shelves, with designer clothes hung above the shoes. Curtis checked behind the shoe rack, finding a few gently used pairs of Timberlands. *Shit. Maybe he has it on him? No. If he's dealing, he wouldn't want to risk being robbed. It has to be here.*

Curtis thought about prom, remembering the time Daryl had smuggled weed into the dance in his shoe. Curtis searched the Air Jordan collection, shoving his hand into each one, but they were clean. He checked the Timberlands. *Got it.* Curtis removed the deposit bag from the boot. It appeared that the money was all there, although Curtis wasn't certain how much money was in there to begin with.

The roar of a V8 engine came from outside. Curtis rushed to the window and parted the blinds. Daryl parked his Chevy Impala SS in the driveway. *Shit.* Curtis scanned the room, his heart thumping in his chest, the deposit bag in his hand. His initial inclination was to hide, but he knew that was stupid because Denise would undoubtedly tell Daryl that Curtis was in his room. Instead, Curtis unlocked the window and pushed upward, but it wouldn't budge. It had been painted shut.

The front door opened and shut. Curtis bent down in an athletic stance and pushed up on the window again, grunting from the effort. The window moved a fraction of an inch, then it broke free from the paint and opened.

Denise tried to talk to her son downstairs, but Daryl said, "I ain't got time for this."

Curtis climbed through the second-floor window and hung from the window frame. He glanced down, eight feet of air between his sneakers and the tiny strip of grass.

The door to Daryl's bedroom flew open, and Curtis let go, falling to the grass, his knees bending with the impact. Curtis ran to his bike and pedaled away.

Daryl shouted from the window. "Curtis!"

Curtis took the long way to Mason's Farm & Feed, using side streets in a zigzag pattern, just in case Daryl gave chase in his car. He parked his bike in front and walked inside with the deposit bag discreetly in hand. To his right, a worker wearing headphones fixed the broken window.

Curtis waited as Fred Mason helped a customer.

"Great day for gardening," Mr. Mason said, handing the woman a plastic bag filled with seed packets. "Enjoy the sunshine."

"I will." The woman took her bag and left.

Mr. Mason smiled at Curtis and said, "Can I help you, young man?"

Curtis was speechless for a second, confused as to why Mr. Mason hadn't remembered him. "Uh, … Mr. Mason. I'm Curtis. I was here with Mary Archer the other day."

Mr. Mason narrowed his eyes, then his jaw tightened. "I ain't got nothin' to say to you."

Curtis looked around, making sure they were alone. Only the window repairman was left, but he was lost in his work and his headphones. "I know you lied about the camera. The police made you delete the footage, didn't they?"

"I don't know what you're talkin' about."

"If you tell me what happened, I might be able to help you get your money back."

Mr. Mason glowered at Curtis. "It was you, wasn't it?"

Curtis drew back. "No, but I know people."

Mr. Mason removed his cell phone from his pocket and opened the old flip phone. "I'm calling the police."

Curtis set the deposit bag on the counter. "Please don't."

Mr. Mason shut his phone and grabbed the deposit bag. He opened it and flipped through the cash inside. "It better all be here."

"I didn't steal your money."

Mr. Mason zipped up the deposit bag. "I might've been born at night, but it wasn't last night."

"Please, Mr. Mason. Luke Archer needs your help. Even if the police took the video, if you saw it, you can testify to that."

"I didn't see nothin'. Get the hell outta my store, before I call the police." Mr. Mason pointed toward the exit. "Go on. *Git.*"

CHAPTER 64: MARY AND THE TRUTH

Mary sat at the kitchen table, steam coming from her scrambled eggs. Abby was nearby, enjoying the motion of her swinging chair. A knock came from the kitchen door. She turned to see Curtis in the door window. She set down her fork and went to the door. Mary opened the door, guarding entry, despite her petite frame.

Curtis dipped his head and said, "I gave the money back to Mr. Mason. I confronted him about the video too, but he won't talk."

Mary stepped aside. "Come in."

Curtis entered her kitchen.

Mary shut the door behind them. "You want some eggs?"

"I ate already," Curtis replied.

Mary sat at the table and ate her breakfast.

Curtis greeted Abby, making faces at her, causing her to giggle. Then he sat across from Mary and said, "I can work today. Whatever you need."

"It's not necessary," Mary replied, stabbing her eggs.

"I feel like you're still mad at me. I wasn't the one who stole the money."

"I'm not mad at you." Mary exhaled. "I think, ... I think I'm losing hope. If the police erased that video, then how can I expect Luke to have a fair trial? Tisha was right. He won't." Mary pushed aside her plate, her appetite gone.

Curtis leaned forward, his elbows on the table. "We can't give up. The stakes are too high."

Mary slumped her shoulders. "I'm not giving up. I just don't know what to do."

"Mr. Mason's lying, and I don't think he'd lie unless there was pressure from the police. If we can get him to testify, the police corruption might be enough reasonable doubt to get Luke acquitted."

"You think I should talk to him again?"

"What do we have to lose? It might be better if you go alone though. I don't think he wants to see my face again."

Mary glanced at Abby, the swinging chair clicking back and forth. "Can you watch Abby?"

***

Mary drove to Mason's Farm & Feed. Inside, one customer picked through the loose seed potatoes. Two more browsed the garden tools. Mary met Mr. Mason at the front counter. His body stiffened as she approached.

"We need to talk," Mary said in a hushed whisper.

"I got nothin' to say to you," Mr. Mason replied.

Mary spoke louder, now unconcerned about politeness. "You lied about the camera."

"I don't know—"

"Stop lying!"

The customer at the seed potatoes turned around.

Mr. Mason opened his mouth to speak, but nothing came out.

Mary took a deep breath, her demeanor softening. "All I'm asking is for you to tell the truth. Please, Mr. Mason."

His eyes were glassy. "I'm sorry. I can't."

"Why not?"

Mr. Mason looked down. "It wouldn't matter. They'll never let Luke go."

CHAPTER 65: CURTIS AND MAKING IT RIGHT

Curtis and Tisha sat at her desk, watching a clip from their documentary on her laptop.

An older man said, "I had a jazz bar in downtown Carville. This was about twenty years ago. It was doing well too. I thought I was on to something big. I had plans to open a second location near Philly." The man took a sip of water. "Then the Carville police started setting up sobriety checks every Friday and Saturday around ten, after most people were drinking, but before most people went home." He shook his head. "They had multiple checkpoints. My customers couldn't leave without hitting a checkpoint. Hundreds of my customers got DUIs. Had their licenses suspended. Lost their jobs if they needed to drive for work." He was quiet for a long moment. Then he said, "Business dried up. I eventually lost everything."

"Do you think racism was involved?" Tisha asked on the video.

He shrugged. "I don't know about that. I do know that we have several Irish bars in Carville. I've never heard of them being hit with sobriety checkpoints. Maybe that's racism, or maybe that's where the police like to drink."

Curtis paused the documentary. "This is really good. I mean, terrible for Mr. Joseph, but good content for the documentary."

Tisha nodded. "He's very credible."

"We have good content, but I feel like we need a headliner. Someone with something *really* big. Something that will grab people's attention."

"We may not find that headliner."

"What do we do if we don't?"

"If we can market it properly, I think it still might work."

"How do you market a documentary?"

Tisha grinned. "Remember that class I took on digital marketing?"

Curtis shook his head, a half smile on his face. "No. I doubt I'd remember the class if *I* took it."

"Lucky for you, I do remember it." She paused for a second. "I think we should release it for free. And I think we should run Facebook ads promoting the video to every person with a Facebook account who lives in Carville and the surrounding areas."

"You can target the ad to go to people around here?"

"Yes. It's super easy."

"Sounds expensive."

"It's not. If we have good engagement, we might pay like ten cents per view."

Curtis drew his eyebrows together. "Depending on how far out of Carville you go, that could be twenty thousand people. At ten cents a click, that's like two grand."

"Don't worry about it. I got a nice donation today."

Curtis leaned away from Tisha. "From who? Your parents?"

"They think it's a good cause. We *are* a nonprofit, so we have to accept charity."

"You're right. I'll have to thank them before I go." Curtis checked the clock on Tisha's laptop—*7:46 p.m.* "I can't believe it's so late. I have to go. I told my dad that I'd bring his truck back by eight."

Tisha raised her eyebrows. "Leonard's going out? Is it a date?"

It was Saturday night.

Curtis smirked. "No. He's playing dominoes with his friends from high school."

"That's nice that he still sees his friends from high school."

Curtis frowned. "Yeah."

Tisha took his hand. "You thinking about Daryl?"

Curtis had already told Tisha about breaking and entering the feedstore and then stealing the money back from Daryl. "I doubt Daryl and I will be playing dominoes in twenty years."

"Well, that's on him, if he wants to act like a thug."

Curtis stood from the desk, letting go of Tisha's hand. He snatched his keys from the desktop. "This didn't start overnight. He did dumb shit when we were young, but I didn't tell him to stop. I thought it was funny. I probably encouraged him. No. That's not true. I *did* encourage him. I smoked weed with him in the bathroom at prom. We stole candy from the corner store. It was like I stopped, but he kept going, and I didn't try to stop him."

Tisha stood from the desk and faced Curtis. "Until now."

"I feel like it's too late now."

Tisha kissed him on the lips. "He'll come around."

"I hope so." Curtis hugged her tight, not letting go for a long time. When they separated, Tisha asked, "What was that for?"

"For being you."

Tisha smiled.

"I'll see you tomorrow."

On his way out, Curtis thanked Tisha's parents for their generous donation. Then he drove from the wealthy enclave of Carville McMansions to his middle-class neighborhood. His dad was waiting in the driveway, as Curtis parked the truck.

Leonard checked his watch, as Curtis met him in the driveway. "You're late."

"By four minutes."

"Six minutes by my watch. If you're not early—"

"You're late." Curtis finished the saying that he'd heard hundreds of times.

Leonard suppressed a smile. "I made spaghetti, if you're hungry."

"Thanks, Dad. Have fun."

Leonard left in his pickup.

Curtis went inside and heated up a bowl of spaghetti in the microwave. After eating, he showered, brushed his teeth, and checked his social media. Shortly thereafter, he drifted off to sleep.

***

Knocking woke Curtis from his slumber. He checked his phone on his bedside table—*11:03 p.m.* The knocking was urgent. *Shit. Mason called the police.* Curtis got up, put on a pair of sweatpants, sneakers, and a T-shirt. More knocking came from the front door.

Curtis stepped down the stairs, his palms sweaty, and his stomach doing somersaults. The knocking ceased. Curtis crept to the front door and peeked out the sidelight window. Nobody was there, but a car drove away, or maybe it was simply passing by. A wave of relief passed over him. He opened the front door and stepped onto the concrete stoop, trying to catch a glimpse of the car, wanting to know if it was the cops. Daryl emerged from the hedge to the right of the door, dressed in all black. He grabbed Curtis by the neck and tossed him to the ground. Curtis landed in the soft, freshly cut grass of the front yard, dimly lit by the porch light.

Two more men emerged from the hedge. Daryl and his two henchmen surrounded Curtis. Curtis rose to one knee.

Daryl said, "Stay down, motherfucker."

Curtis showed his palms. "I'm sorry, Daryl. I did what I thought was right."

Daryl chuckled, glancing at his henchmen, who also chuckled. "Listen to this punk-ass nigga. Doin' what's right? With *my* money?"

Curtis recognized the other men as local drug dealers and all-around criminals, who were a few years older than he and Daryl.

Daryl glared at Curtis. "Where's my fuckin' money?"

"It's gone. I gave it back," Curtis replied.

Daryl threw a roundhouse right that connected just below Curtis's eye. Curtis sprawled on his side, seeing stars. The three men then kicked and stomped Curtis with their boots. Curtis covered his head, contorting his body away from each blow. The roar of a truck engine raced toward them. Headlights lit the scene. Leonard and his pickup truck hopped the curb and drove on his manicured lawn, coming to a screeching halt mere feet from the melee.

The beating stopped, the men frozen like deer in the headlights. Leonard exited the truck and fired his pistol into the air. The three men scattered like roaches, sprinting for Daryl's Impala, which had been parked a few houses down.

Leonard holstered his weapon and rushed to Curtis's side. "Are you okay?"

"I think so." Curtis groaned and tried to rise to his feet.

Leonard helped his son to stand. "Let's get you inside."

Curtis put his arm around his father, letting Leonard help him inside. Curtis's ribs ached, and blood slipped down his face from the cut beneath his eye. Leonard helped Curtis to the couch in the living room.

Leonard flipped on the light, inspected Curtis's face, and said, "Where does it hurt?"

"My ribs hurt when I move, but I think they're just bruised."

"I'll be right back." Leonard rushed outside, and returned with the first-aid kit he kept in his vehicle. Leonard set the kit on the coffee table, went to the kitchen, and returned with some warm water and a towel. Leonard dipped the towel in the warm water and cleaned the blood from Curtis's face. "What the hell was that about? I saw Daryl."

"He's pissed at me," Curtis replied.

Leonard arched his eyebrows, standing over Curtis. "That's an understatement."

"Daryl stole some money, and I took it from him to give it back."

Leonard drew back and stared at his son, the wheels turning in his mind. "The feedstore."

Curtis nodded. "Fred Mason deleted the camera footage from May seventh."

"The day Luke Archer killed Lambert."

"Yeah. I wanted to get the footage. It could save Luke. I think the police made him delete the footage."

Leonard scowled at his son. "You broke into the feedstore."

Curtis swallowed hard. "I wasn't there to steal anything. I just wanted the camera footage."

Leonard dipped a cotton swab in alcohol and cleaned Curtis's cut.

Curtis winced.

Leonard applied a fresh Band-Aid, then he said, "Did you give Fred Mason his money back?"

"Yes, sir."

Leonard let out a heavy breath. "God *damn*, boy. You can't be doin' shit like that. You're gonna get arrested or *worse*. Hell, you could be dead right now, if I hadn't come home when I did."

Curtis hung his head. "I know. I'm sorry, Dad. I'm just trying to make it right."

Leonard put his hand on Curtis's shoulder and squeezed. "I know you are, son, and I've never been prouder."

Curtis looked up at his father. "You're proud of me?"

Leonard nodded. "Do me a favor though. Stick to helpin' out on the farm."

"Okay."

"We should go to the hospital."

"I'm fine, Dad. Really."

"Humor me. Let's at least get you some X-rays."

CHAPTER 66: LIZZIE, TWO WEEKS LATER

The sun was high and bright overhead. Lizzie sat under the umbrella of her patio table, an iced tea in hand, watching Emma play in the backyard with her Hula-Hoop. The sliding glass door opened and shut behind her.

Lizzie turned to see her son. "Hey, honey."

"Can I go over to Jeremy's?" Brian asked, sidling up to Lizzie.

"Do you need a ride?"

"I can ride my bike."

"Okay, but I have three conditions."

Brian slumped his shoulders. "Aw. Come on, Mom."

Lizzie set her tea on the table and held up one finger. "Number one. I need you home by seven. I'm grilling burgers."

"With fries?" Brian asked, perking up.

"With fries." Lizzie held up two fingers. "Number two. I need you to be careful. Watch out for cars."

"Okay."

Lizzie held up three fingers. "Number three. I need a hug."

Brian bent over and hugged his mother.

Lizzie kissed him on the cheek and said, "I love you."

Brian wiggled out of the hug. "Bye, Mom." He ran toward the front yard.

Lizzie felt the sting of the unrequited *I love you*, but Brian stopped about twenty feet away, turned to Lizzie, and called out, "Love you too, Mom." Then he ran for his bike.

Lizzie smiled to herself and went back to watching Emma, trying to twirl the Hula-Hoop. Lizzie walked over to Emma, offering encouragement and coaching. When Emma improved just a little by gyrating her hips,

Lizzie clapped, as if it had been the greatest accomplishment in the world. Emma beamed at the attention. They played until a police SUV parked in their driveway.

Dennis walked into her backyard and called out to Lizzie in a stern voice, "I need to talk to you."

Lizzie addressed Emma. "Mommy will be right back."

"Okay," Emma replied, still gyrating with her Hula-Hoop.

Lizzie walked across the lawn to Dennis, her face like stone. "Get off my property."

Dennis grabbed her by the elbow and led her through the sliding glass door and into the living room.

Once inside, Lizzie jerked her arm away from Dennis.

Dennis shut the door behind them. "Why the *hell* are you talking to Gina Walters?"

Lizzie spoke matter-of-factly. "None of your business."

"You think you can testify about what Brad did to you? Judge Malone will never allow it."

Lizzie shrugged, enjoying her position of perceived power, even though she had no intention of testifying. "Like I said, it's none of your business."

Dennis crowded her, his face inches from hers. "Don't play coy with me."

Lizzie didn't back down. She enunciated perfectly. "Fuck. You."

Dennis clenched his fists, his face reddening. "I can make your life very difficult."

"I'm late."

Dennis took a step back. "What the hell are you talking about?"

"You heard me. I'm late."

Dennis ran his hand over his face. "God damn it." He walked away from Lizzie toward the dark television.

Lizzie followed. "You don't have to be a father, but you *will* pay child support."

He turned around and faced her, his lips curled into a sneer. "If you're pregnant, which I doubt, *get rid of it.*"

"No."

Dennis grabbed her by the shoulders. "You'll do what I fucking tell you to do."

"Fuck you."

Dennis reared back and slapped her in the face.

The sting was instant. Lizzie tilted her head, touched her red cheek, and said, "Get out."

Dennis grabbed her by the shoulders again, squeezing like a vise, and shaking her. "You think you're gonna hold me hostage with this baby?"

Lizzie spat in his face, the ball of saliva landing on the tip of his nose, and splattering across his face.

Dennis let go and stepped back. He wiped his face and glared at Lizzie, with one side of his mouth raised in disgust.

Lizzie had seen that look many times before from Brad. She cowered and covered her face with her arms, bracing herself for the inevitable impact.

Dennis reared back again, but this time he punched her in the lower abdomen, dropping Lizzie like a stone. He left her on the floor gasping for air. When her wind returned, intense cramps came from her lower stomach. She struggled to her feet, the cramps intensifying. She staggered down the hall to the bathroom.

Lizzie pulled down her pants. Blood stained her underwear.

Chapter 67: Lizzie and DA Perkins

Lizzie sat in the chair across from DA Perkins at his dark mahogany desk, wincing, her stomach still sore from the punch she'd absorbed last week. Bookshelves filled with legal texts lined the walls. The DA wore a white button-down shirt, the sleeves rolled up to his elbows.

He said, "What can I do for you, Mrs. Lambert?"

Lizzie took a deep breath and said, "I'd like to report an assault."

He leaned back in his leather chair. "Chief Rhodes?"

Lizzie was stunned for a beat. "Yes. How did you know?"

"Chief Rhodes already told me everything."

"He did?"

Perkins nodded. "He did. Affairs can be very messy. They can make people do things that they wouldn't normally do. Don't you agree?"

"Yes. They are messy, but this isn't about the affair."

"I know," DA Perkins replied, stroking his chin.

"You do?"

"I know all about the blackmail."

Lizzie drew back. "Blackmail? What are you talking about?"

DA Perkins leaned forward, placing his elbows on the desk. "I sympathize with you, Mrs. Lambert. I really do. I know you've been through a lot. I understand why you fixated on Chief Rhodes."

"*Fixated?*"

"Maybe that's the wrong word. You needed someone after the tragedy. I understand. I really do. However, you can't blackmail a man because he no longer wants to be with you."

Lizzie twisted her face in anger. "*What?* I never blackmailed anyone. He choked me. He punched me in the stomach. I lost my child because of him."

Perkins narrowed his eyes. "Is there any evidence of this?"

"*Yes.* I'm telling you what happened. My stomach's still sore. I'm sure the hospital can verify that I was pregnant, and I've had trauma."

"Chief Rhodes describes the situation far differently."

Lizzie leaned forward, on the edge of her seat. "I'm telling the truth."

"A case is only as good as the evidence. I've already talked to a witness who described in detail how you paid him to punch you in the stomach, so you could then blackmail Chief Rhodes."

Lizzie held out her hands. "Why the hell would I do that? If I wanted to blackmail him, I would've used our baby."

"That's the thing. Chief Rhodes doesn't believe it was his baby. According to him, you're seeing several men."

Lizzie shot out of her seat, her face beet red. "That's a lie."

Perkins shrugged. "How do I know that? As a prosecutor, what I have is a he-said, she-said situation. The only evidence is the man you hired to punch you in the stomach. At this point, I can't prosecute Chief Rhodes, but I could prosecute you."

Lizzie trembled with rage.

"I'd rather not go down that road because I know how much you've suffered. I suggest you move on with your life and leave Chief Rhodes to repair his marriage."

Lizzie pointed at the DA, her finger shaking. "You're … You're …" She was at a loss for words, so she pivoted and left the office, leaving the door open in her wake.

Tears streamed down her face as she fast-walked to the elevator. Two paralegals waited for the elevator, so Lizzie took the stairs to the ground floor, not wanting the women to notice her distress. Then she hurried from the building to the parking lot.

In her SUV, she hung her head and bawled like a baby. When the tears finally went dry, she rifled through her purse for a business card. She stared at the name on the card—Gina Walters—for a long time. Then she tapped the number.

CHAPTER 68: CURTIS, SIX MONTHS LATER

Curtis hauled boxes of potatoes, winter squash, and sorrel to the truck. It was the last CSA delivery of the growing season. Curtis had already committed in his mind to helping Mary for as long as she needed, even if that meant the duration of a twenty-five-year prison sentence. Luke's trial was next week, so Curtis would learn of his self-imposed sentence soon enough. He shut the tailgate and blew out a breath of condensed air. *Please, God. Let Luke go free.* Curtis wasn't a religious man, but Mary had rubbed off on him.

He walked back to the farmhouse and stuck his head into the kitchen. "Truck's loaded. I'm headed out."

Mary sat at the kitchen table, writing checks, and balancing the books. Abby lay in the nearby playpen, kicking her arms and legs at the rotating mobile. Mary set down her pen, checked the clock on the stove, and said, "Could you come in here for second?"

Curtis stepped into the kitchen, letting a blast of cold air in with him. "What's up?"

Mary stood from the table, meeting Curtis in the middle of the kitchen. She handed him an envelope.

Curtis took the envelope with a creased brow. "What's this?"

"I wish it could be more."

Curtis opened the envelope to find a check for four grand. "Mary, this isn't necessary." He handed back the check.

Mary wouldn't take it. "It is. If not for you, I would've lost the farm."

"But—"

"No buts." Mary gestured to the papers on her desk. "I did the math. We have enough money to make it through the winter, even if we don't sell microgreens."

Curtis tried to give the check back again. "You might need this money."

Mary shook her head. "Please take it."

"Thank you."

Mary stepped closer to Curtis and hugged him tight. When they separated, she said, "You're a good friend, Curtis. I wish it never happened, but I'm glad we met."

CHAPTER 69: MARY AND THE COMMONWEALTH'S CASE, DAY ONE

The first witness hadn't been a witness at all. Sergeant Geoff Collins, the man in charge of the bodycam footage for the Carville County Police Department, had been questioned by DA Alex Perkins. Based on the sergeant's testimony, the DA had established that the bodycam footage was self-authenticating and, therefore, admitted into evidence.

The jury initially saw a very short version of the video, starting with Luke taking Officer Lambert's baton, then hitting the officer across the temple. The audible *crack*, shown several times, caused many on the jury to wince. DA Perkins had paused the video, showing Luke towering over Officer Lambert, the baton held high, ready to strike, Luke's face contorted and beet red. Mary had looked away from the image, but it was burned into her memory. There was no evidence from the footage that Officer Lambert drew his weapon.

During cross-examination, defense attorney Gina Walters, had shown the rest of the video, adding important context. The jury saw Curtis Mays antagonize Officer Lambert, then the ensuing verbal argument, followed by Curtis spitting. Curtis had clearly turned his head to spit, although it wasn't impossible that some saliva had landed on Officer Lambert, as he had claimed in the video.

Curtis had appeared to resist arrest, and Lambert beat him with an intensity that made the jury wince again. Then Luke was heard yelling for Officer Lambert to stop. When he didn't, Luke, the three-hundred-pound behemoth, had slammed into Officer Lambert, knocking him to the ground and off Curtis.

Officer Lambert had risen to his feet and ordered Luke to the ground. When Luke didn't comply, Lambert attacked Luke with his baton. Gina Walters had paused the video, showing Officer Lambert with a contorted red-faced expression, his baton raised, resembling the image of Luke that DA Perkins had shown.

Mary sat in the front-row pew, with Curtis and Tisha, behind the defense table. Luke and Gina Walters whispered back and forth. It was a ten-minute recess now. Mary wondered if they were discussing the bodycam footage. From Mary's uneducated perspective, Gina had done a good job, making sure the jury saw the context around the event, but that didn't change the law.

In the opening statements, DA Perkins had claimed that the law was on their side, that Lambert had been making a lawful arrest.

The audience filtered back into the courtroom. Like during the preliminary hearing, the pews were crowded with police officers. Curtis waved toward a balding man with a gray beard. The man waved back and found one of the last open seats toward the back.

"Who's that?" Mary asked.

Curtis turned to Mary. "My dad."

"That's nice of him to come."

Counting Curtis's father, only four people were in the audience for Luke.

The courtroom clerk returned from recess, followed by the judge. Judge Harry Malone sat behind his desk on high. The courtroom clerk sat to the judge's left, behind a shorter desk. Deputies were strategically positioned around the packed courtroom. The judge called the courtroom to order.

DA Perkins called Officer Larry Dunne to the stand, the first officer on the scene after Officer Lambert was killed. The doughy police officer was sworn in. DA Perkins asked a series of questions, establishing Dunne's identity and credibility. Then Larry Dunne described his experience on May 7. His testimony hadn't deviated from the preliminary hearing. Luke had been standing in the parking lot in a trance, holding the bloody police baton.

DA Perkins finished his questioning by asking, "When you saw Officer Lambert lying on the macadam, do you remember seeing his gun?"

Officer Dunne nodded, his voice confident. "Yes, I do."

"Where was his gun?"

"In his holster."

CHAPTER 70: CURTIS AND THE COMMONWEALTH'S CASE, DAY TWO

In the morning, DA Perkins questioned the medical examiner, establishing Officer Lambert's cause of death as blunt force trauma. He also questioned a woman from the Pennsylvania State Police Crime Lab to confirm that Luke's fingerprints were on the baton or murder weapon and that the blood on the end of it was in fact Officer Lambert's. Gina hadn't bothered to cross-examine either of these witnesses.

Detective Lee Armstrong was on the witness stand now—tall and well-built, with a strong chin. He resembled a superhero. Curtis remembered the man from *his* interrogation.

DA Perkins stood at the podium between the defense and prosecution tables. He asked, "Did you interview the defendant, after he was apprehended on May seventh, 2021?"

"Yes," Detective Armstrong replied.

"Would you recognize printed transcripts of your interview with the defendant?"

"I would."

"Would the transcripts be helpful to answer questions regarding that interview?"

"They would."

Perkins picked up a stack of papers from the podium and addressed Judge Malone. "I have copies of the interview transcripts. This is the Commonwealth's exhibit sixteen. May I approach the witness for authentication?"

"You may," Judge Malone replied.

DA Perkins handed a copy to Gina Walters at the defense table, then another copy to the clerk, before giving Detective Armstrong a copy on the witness stand. Perkins kept one copy for himself. "Can you identify exhibit sixteen for the court?"

Detective Armstrong flipped through the transcripts for a minute. Then he looked up and said, "These are the transcripts from my interview with Luke Archer on May seventh."

"Do they appear to be accurate?"

"Yes."

Perkins addressed Judge Malone. "Your Honor, we offer the Commonwealth's exhibit sixteen into evidence at this time. The authenticity has been affirmed."

Judge Malone addressed Gina. "Any objection?"

Gina stayed seated. "No, Your Honor."

"Commonwealth's exhibit sixteen is admitted into evidence."

Perkins nodded to the judge, returned to the podium, then addressed his witness again. "Detective Armstrong, would you please turn to page two of the interview transcript."

The detective flipped to page two.

"I've highlighted part of the interview. Your questions are in yellow highlighter, and the defendant's answers are in purple. Please read the first sentence in yellow."

Detective Armstrong nodded and read from the page. "Why did you hit Officer Lambert with the baton?"

Perkins read silently from the transcript, keeping pace with the detective. "Now please read the response of the defendant."

The detective read Luke's part without emotion. "He was reaching for his gun. It all happened so fast. I was scared."

Perkins prompted Armstrong to read his next line.

"Are you sure he drew his weapon? The bodycam footage doesn't show that."

Perkins prompted Armstrong to read Luke's reply.

"I, … I don't know. I thought he was reaching for his gun."

Perkins prompted Armstrong again.

"Police officers can and do draw their weapons to stop an attack. Do you think Officer Lambert just wanted you to drop the baton?"

"How did the defendant reply?" Perkins asked.

Detective Armstrong cleared his throat. "He said, 'I don't know. I was afraid he'd kill me, like the man he was beating.'"

"Please read your reply."

"That man's alive and well. His name's Curtis Mays. At the time you hit Officer Lambert with the baton, did you believe Curtis Mays was in fact dead?"

Perkins prompted Armstrong to read Luke's reply.

"I didn't know."

Perkins prompted Armstrong to read his next question.

"Did you know that Curtis routinely agitates police officers and interferes with traffic stops and routine investigations? He runs a YouTube channel called Carville Cop Watch."

"Objection. Relevancy," Gina said, sitting at the defense table.

Murmurs came from the officers in the audience. Juror number five, a dead ringer for Martha Stewart, scowled at Luke.

"Sustained. Stay on task, Counselor," Judge Malone said to DA Perkins.

Curtis felt like the police officers in the audience were staring daggers into his back. He glanced back, catching more than a few glares from the audience, but also seeing a surprising yet familiar face. Fred Mason sat in the back, sandwiched between two uniformed officers.

"Please read the next highlighted question in yellow," DA Perkins said.

The detective said, "Do you really believe Officer Lambert would've killed you if you would've dropped that baton? A decorated officer who has never shot anyone?"

DA Perkins glanced at the jury and asked, "What was the defendant's response?"

"It was a mistake. I'm so sorry."

"Please read your final question for the defendant."

"You didn't answer my question." Detective Armstrong looked up from his paper, knowing the subsequent words by heart, and staring at DA Perkins with the same intensity that Curtis imagined he had used against Luke. "Do you believe Officer Lambert would've killed you if you didn't hit him in the head and kill him first?"

"And what was the defendant's response?" Perkins turned to the jury, with raised eyebrows.

Detective Armstrong replied, "The defendant said, 'No.'"

A few jurors scribbled notes. Curtis wondered if they were writing, *guilty.*

Perkins turned back to the detective. "To the best of your recollection, does this transcript accurately reflect your interview with the defendant on May seventh, 2021?"

The detective nodded. "Yes, it does."

More than a few jurors nodded, along with the detective.

CHAPTER 71: MARY AND FIGHTING

At the end of the second day of the trial, Mary walked to the courthouse parking lot, hugging her coat tight around her. Winter wind whistled past the gothic building. She was surrounded by Curtis, Tisha, and Leonard—Curtis's father. They made sure the local media, and the small crowd of Blue Lives Matter supporters kept their distance.

Once Mary was safely in her pickup truck, her protectors left her for their own vehicles. One by one, Mary watched the vehicles leave the parking lot. She thought about the trial and the fact that they were clearly losing. Nobody said as much. Curtis and Tisha tried to be positive, but Mary knew the truth. Once she felt like she had a modicum of privacy, she lay her head on the steering wheel and sobbed. She cried for Luke. She cried for herself. Most of all she cried for Abby.

A tap at her window jolted her upright. Mary wiped her face with her sleeve and rolled down the window.

"Are you okay?" Mr. Mason asked.

Mary's face hardened. "No. I'm *not* okay. Why would I be?"

Mr. Mason bowed his head. "I'm sorry, Mary—"

"What are you sorry for? That you won't help Luke? What do you know?"

Mr. Mason glanced over his shoulder, spotting a nearby police cruiser. "I'm sorry, Mary. I can't." Mr. Mason hurried to his pickup truck.

Mary exited her truck and chased Mr. Mason, pelting the old man's back with her rapid-fire questions. "Are you afraid of the police? Did they tell you to delete the video? Please Mr. Mason. If you know something…"

Mr. Mason turned around at his truck to face Mary. "Doesn't matter. It's gone."

Mary held out her hands like a beggar. "Please, Mr. Mason."

"I'm sorry." Mr. Mason climbed into his truck.

Mary knocked on his truck window. "Please, Mr. Mason."

The old man started his truck and drove away, not making eye contact with Mary.

Mary ran back to her truck, jumped in the driver's seat, and drove after Mr. Mason. She followed him out of town, keeping her distance, hoping to surprise him. Mary drove on a curvy country road, gripping the steering wheel with white knuckles.

Thirteen minutes later, Mr. Mason turned into a rural neighborhood of fifties-built homes. He parked his truck in front of a redbrick rambler. Mary parked right behind him. Leaves covered the front yard, courtesy of two large oaks. Mary met the old man in the driveway.

Mr. Mason frowned, his shoulders hunched, as if weighted down by the world. "Go home, Mary."

Mary clasped her hands together, as if she were praying. "Please talk to me. I'm begging you to help me."

"I've already said too much. You need to go home."

"I'm not leaving until you talk to me."

A car drove past, the driver gawking at them.

Mr. Mason let out a long breath. "Park your truck down the street and walk back. They can't know you're here."

"The police?"

"Yeah."

Mary parked on the shoulder around the corner and walked back to his house.

Mr. Mason opened the front door before Mary had a chance to knock. He ushered her inside. The living room was dim with weathered furniture. Stacks of newspapers sat along the wall. Mr. Mason led Mary to the kitchen table. Dishes cluttered the sink and countertops. Scuffs and boot prints marred the white tile floor.

They sat across from each other at the kitchen table.

Mary asked, "What happened to the video? Did the police make you erase it?"

He nodded. "Chief Rhodes made me do it."

Mary slumped her shoulders. "I'm guessing you don't have a copy?"

Mr. Mason shook his head. "I told you. It's gone."

"Did you watch the video before you erased it? If you saw what happened, you could testify ..."

"I didn't watch it, but ..." Mr. Mason pressed his lips together, as if trying to keep his words from spilling out.

Mary leaned forward, with bated breath.

"I saw what happened from the window."

"What did you see?"

"It won't make no difference. If the cops want you, they'll *git* you."

"Please, Mr. Mason. You're the only one who can help us."

He scratched his beard, silent for a long moment.

"Mr. Mason?"

The old man held up his hand. "I'm thinkin'. My memory ain't what it used to be."

Mary wondered if he was making an excuse not to help.

Then he said, "I heard Luke hollerin' at Officer Lambert. That's when I went to the window. That black fella was on the macadam. Wasn't movin'. I thought he was dead. Lambert did draw his gun. That's when Luke hit him. But that ain't the worst part. The first officer who got there ... What's his name?"

"Officer Dunne."

"Yeah. Him. He took the gun from Lambert's hand and put it in his holster."

Mary sucked in a sharp breath. "They're lying."

"And Luke's in this mess, and there ain't no way out."

"You could testify," Mary said, the excitement back in her voice.

"It's too late."

"It might not be."

Mr. Mason shook his head again. "Don't matter. I can't do it."

"Why not?"

He gestured to a picture on his fridge of himself flanked by a middle-aged woman and man. "That's my daughter, Janine, and my son, Fred Jr. Janine runs a day care. Her husband ain't worth a damn. She's keepin' her family afloat damn near on her own. I try to help when I can, but business ain't been good since Tractor Supply and Wal-Mart came to Carville." He paused, catching his breath. "My son's a landscaper. A damn good one too. His business is small, but it's enough to take care of his family."

Mr. Mason pointed to another picture on his fridge of Fred Jr. with a middle-aged woman, surrounded by six teenagers. "That's my son's family. Six kids. The twins will be at Penn State next year. I doubt they can send 'em all to school though—"

"I'm sorry for their struggles," Mary said, interrupting, "but what does this have to do with helping Luke? We don't need money from you. I just want you to tell the truth."

He sucked air through his teeth. "Janine runs her day care out of her home. Junior runs his business out of his garage. Problem is, neither of them are zoned to run those businesses out of their homes. Hell, the feedstore's zoned ag. Technically, we're not allowed to have a storefront, but we've been there forever, so nobody said nothin'."

"Did somebody say something?" Mary asked.

"I've been strugglin' with this. I did what I was told. Lambert was dead, then Chief Rhodes was in my office, wantin' to see the video." Mr. Mason hung his head, staring at the tabletop. "He told me to delete it, so I did. Then he said, if I talked about it, he'd enforce the zonin' on me and my kids." Mr. Mason raised his gaze, peering into Mary's eyes. "I'm sorry. I was hopin' Luke would get off without my testimony."

"He won't." Mary looked at the pictures on the fridge again. She peered at the picture of Mr. Mason smiling, his arm around an older frail woman. Mary pointed to the picture. "Is that your wife?"

Mr. Mason nodded. "She died three years ago. Breast cancer. Fought it tooth and nail to the bitter end. She was a fighter."

"I'm sorry."

"Me too."

"What do you think she'd want you to do?"

He stared at the picture for a long time. Then he turned to Mary and said, "She'd wanna fight like hell. Would've been spittin' mad at Chief Rhodes. Would've told the whole town."

"You still can."

"I don't care about what Rhodes would do to me, but my kids …"

Mary pursed her lips, thinking of a compromise. "What if you only testified about what you saw between Luke and Officer Lambert? You don't have to mention Chief Rhodes or Officer Dunne."

Mr. Mason stroked his beard. "No. If I'm gonna do this, it ain't gonna be half-assed."

CHAPTER 72: LUKE AND THE DEFENSE'S CASE, DAY ONE

Luke looked over his shoulder at Mary, directly behind him, in the first row of the audience. He mouthed, *Thank you.* She smiled. Luke faced forward again, aware of Gina's instructions. *Pay attention and don't show any emotion.* His thank-you was for the witness, who was being sworn in by the judge.

Fred Mason sat in the witness box, his hair and beard disheveled, but he did wear a rumpled suit. Luke suppressed a smile, vindicated in his belief that Officer Lambert did draw his weapon. Gina had tried to acquire Officer Dunne's bodycam footage to show him holstering Lambert's handgun, but Dunne's camera had apparently malfunctioned on May 7. This was disappointing and likely another example of corruption, but Luke concentrated on what they did have. Mr. Mason's eyewitness testimony.

"What made you go to the window?" Gina asked from the podium, between the prosecution and defense tables.

Mr. Mason leaned into the mike. "I heard Luke hollerin' in the parking lot."

"Did you hear what he said?"

"No, ma'am. Just heard him shoutin'."

"Did you look out the window?"

"Yes, ma'am. I did."

Gina checked the jury, making sure they were engaged before proceeding. "What did you see?"

"I saw Officer Lambert beatin' an unconscious man."

Murmurs came from the sea of blue in the audience.

"What happened after that?" Gina asked.

Mr. Mason cleared his throat and replied, "Luke ran over and hit Officer Lambert, not with his fist, but with his body, like he was a football player. Lambert got up and started hittin' Luke with his stick. Then Luke took the stick. Lambert drew his gun, but Luke hit him on the head before he could point it at him."

Luke glanced at the jury. They appeared engaged, two nodding along with Mr. Mason, but the foreman—a Paul Bunyan look-alike—glared with eyes as black as coal, his arms crossed over his chest.

"Do you think Luke intended to kill Officer Lambert?" Gina asked.

"Objection. Speculation," DA Perkins said from his seat at the prosecution table.

"I'll rephrase." Gina paused for a beat, then asked, "Did it look to you like Luke was trying to kill Officer Lambert?"

"No, ma'am. It didn't," Mr. Mason replied.

"How do you know that?"

"Because Luke only hit Officer Lambert once."

More murmurs came from the audience.

Gina waited for the audience to quiet. "Do you have security cameras at your place of business?"

"Yes, ma'am. I do," Mr. Mason replied.

"Did one of your security cameras record the altercation on May seventh between Luke Archer and Officer Lambert?"

"Yes, ma'am."

"Do you have that video in your possession?"

"No, ma'am."

"Why not?"

"Because Chief Rhodes made me erase it."

DA Perkins sprang from his seat. "*Objection.*"

The courtroom erupted with jeers.

Judge Malone banged his gavel. "Order. Order in the court."

When the audience quieted, DA Perkins said, "This testimony is hearsay, Your Honor."

"The witness didn't testify about anything that the chief said." Gina gestured to DA Perkins. "Of course, the DA is free to cross-examine the witness on this point."

"Overruled," Judge Malone said.

DA Perkins clenched his jaw.

Gina stifled a smirk. "Thank you, Mr. Mason. No further questions."

DA Alex Perkins replaced Gina at the podium for his cross-examination of Mr. Mason.

"Good morning, Mr. Mason," DA Perkins said.

Mr. Mason leaned into the mike. "Mornin'."

"How far away were you when you witnessed the altercation between the defendant and Officer Lambert?"

Mr. Mason tilted his head. "Not sure. Maybe twenty feet."

"Would it surprise you if I told you that Officer Lambert's body was found exactly forty-three feet away from your store?"

"No. Not really."

"Given that Officer Lambert was over double the distance from you that you thought, do you think it's possible that you're mistaken about Officer Lambert drawing his weapon?"

Mr. Mason swallowed hard. "That's what I saw."

DA Perkins asked, "Were there any customers in your store at the time of the altercation between the defendant and Officer Lambert?"

"I, ... I don't remember."

"When you looked out the window at the altercation between the defendant and Officer Lambert, did you notice any vehicles in your parking lot?"

"I, ... I don't remember."

"You testified"—Perkins read from his notes—"that Luke ran over and hit Officer Lambert, not with his fist, but with his body, like he was a football player. Is that correct?"

"Yes, sir."

"What happened after that?"

"Officer Lambert hit Luke with his stick."

"Did Officer Lambert say anything to Luke prior to hitting him with his stick?"

Mr. Mason furrowed his brow. "I don't remember."

"Would it surprise you to know that the bodycam footage and audio shows Officer Lambert ordering the defendant to the ground, not once, but twice, before ever using any force against the defendant?"

"I, uh ..."

"You remember Officer Lambert drawing a gun from forty-two feet away, but you don't remember if a customer was in your store, if a single vehicle was in your parking lot, or Officer Lambert ordering the defendant to the ground? Your memory is awfully convenient for the defense."

"Objection. Argumentative," Gina Walters said from the defense table.

"Sustained," Judge Malone said. "Move along, Counselor."

"When did this altercation between Officer Lambert and the defendant occur?" DA Perkins asked, his tone harsh.

Mr. Mason glanced at Gina Walters for answers she couldn't give. "I think in the morning."

"Do you remember the date?"

"Uh, … I think it was the eleventh."

"Of what month?"

"I think July? It was warm."

"How about the year? Was it this year? Last year? The year before?"

"Uh, … it was, uh, …." Mr. Mason looked to Gina again for help, but she simply stared back. "It was last year, … I think."

Gina winced.

Luke clenched his fists under the table.

"Two thousand twenty then?"

Mr. Mason nodded. "Yes."

DA Perkins nodded to the jury, then addressed the witness again. "This altercation took place on May seventh, 2021, seven months ago."

Mr. Mason dipped his head. "I meant this year."

"Did you tell your wife about what you witnessed on May seventh of 2021?"

"Objection. Relevance," Gina said.

DA Perkins flashed his palms to the judge. "It goes to competency, Your Honor."

"Overruled, but don't stray too far."

"Thank you, Your Honor."

"Answer the question, Mr. Mason," Judge Malone said.

"What was the question?" Mr. Mason asked.

"Did you tell your wife about the altercation between Officer Lambert and the defendant that you witnessed on May seventh of 2021?" DA Perkins asked.

Mr. Mason scanned the courtroom again, a blank look on his face.

"Mr. Mason? Did you tell your wife about what you saw on May seventh of 2021?"

"I, … I don't remember, but I must've told her. She's my best friend. Do you know where she is?"

Luke looked down, not wanting to witness Mr. Mason's humiliation and his own downfall in real time.

DA Perkins checked the jury, then addressed the witness. "Mr. Mason, I'm sorry to tell you this, but your wife's been dead for three years."

Hushed whispers came from the audience.

Tears welled in Mr. Mason's eyes.

DA Perkins continued. "How are we supposed to trust your account of the altercation on May seventh when you don't even know what year it transpired? You can't recall major details, like Officer Lambert's lawful orders given to the defendant, how close you were to the scene, whether or not vehicles were in the parking lot, whether or not customers were in your store. You can't even remember whether or not your spouse is still alive."

"Objection, Your Honor. Argumentative," Gina said from the defense table.

A tear disappeared into Mr. Mason's beard.

Luke glanced at the jury again. Their engagement was now mostly directed at DA Perkins. A few scowled at Luke and the defense table.

"I'll withdrawal it," DA Perkins said, with a wave of his hand. "No further questions."

***

After lunch, Curtis Mays sat in the witness box, wearing a well-fitted dark suit. He told Gina Walters and the jury about the argument he had had with Officer Lambert.

"Did you spit on Officer Lambert?" Gina asked from the podium.

"No," Curtis replied. "I turned my head and spat on the ground."

"What happened after you spat on the ground?"

"Officer Lambert grabbed me and threw me to the ground. He wrenched my arm behind my back. He beat me with his baton, which really hurt."

"Where did he hit you?"

"Across my back mostly, but he did hit me on the back of my head. Right here." Curtis touched the spot on his head. "That knocked me unconscious."

"If Luke Archer hadn't intervened, do you think Officer Lambert would've killed you?"

DA Perkins sprang from his seat. "Objection. Speculative."

"Your Honor, the witness's state of mind at the time of the event is not speculation," Gina said.

"It is when he's unconscious," DA Perkins added.

"Sustained," Judge Malone said.

"Yes. Lambert would've killed me," Curtis said.

Judge Malone banged his gavel and glared at Curtis. "The witness will not answer." The judge addressed the jury. "The jury will *disregard* the last statement by the witness." Then he pointed his gavel at Gina Walters. "Control your witness, Counselor."

CHAPTER 73: LUKE AND THE DEFENSE'S CASE, DAY TWO

Sensing that they were losing the trial, Luke had begged Gina to put him on the stand, so he could tell his story. She had reluctantly agreed, acknowledging that it probably wouldn't hurt in this case. Luke had taken that to mean that the trial was already a disaster, so how could it possibly get any worse.

"I saw Officer Lambert beating Curtis Mays unconscious with his stick," Luke said, sitting on the witness stand next to Judge Malone.

"How did you know that Curtis was unconscious?" Gina asked from the podium.

"I didn't know for sure, but he wasn't moving."

"What happened next?"

"I yelled at Officer Lambert. I said, 'Hey. He's not moving.'"

"How did Officer Lambert react to that?"

"He didn't. He just kept hitting Curtis."

Gina glanced at the jury, letting them process Luke's testimony. "What happened next?"

"I ran over there and rammed into Officer Lambert, knocking him off Curtis."

"Did you intend to hurt Officer Lambert?"

Luke shook his head as he said, "Absolutely not."

"What happened after you knocked Officer Lambert off of Curtis Mays?"

"Officer Lambert got up again, and he was angry."

"How did you know he was angry?"

"His face was red, and he yelled at me, using profanity. He pointed his stick at me and told me to get on the *f-ing* ground."

"Did you lay on the ground as Officer Lambert ordered?" Gina asked.

"No, I didn't."

"Why not?"

Luke wrung his hands in his lap, as he said, "I was worried that he'd beat me like he did Curtis."

"What happened when you disobeyed Officer Lambert's order?" Gina asked.

"Officer Lambert hit me on the side of my knee with his stick. Then he tried to hit me in the head, but I grabbed his stick and took it from him." Luke took a deep breath. "Then he grabbed his gun. That's when I hit him."

"Did you intend to kill Officer Lambert?"

Luke shook his head again. "No. I just didn't want him to shoot me."

"Were you afraid for your life?"

"Yes. Yes, I was."

"No further questions," Gina said.

Luke checked the jury. They mostly appeared neutral except for the foreman, who again glared at Luke. Luke shifted his gaze back to the podium.

DA Perkins replaced Gina Walters at the podium for cross-examination. "Good morning."

Luke nodded back.

DA Perkins addressed Judge Malone. "May I approach the witness? I have questions that pertain to evidence."

"You may," Judge Malone replied.

Perkins walked to the evidence table to the left of Judge Malone. He picked up the transcript from the police interview. DA Perkins held it up and said, "Commonwealth's exhibit number sixteen." As he passed Gina and the defense table, Perkins showed her the exhibit he was holding.

Gina nodded in response.

DA Perkins handed the exhibit to Luke, keeping a copy for himself. "Are these the transcripts from your police interview with Detective Armstrong on May seventh of 2021?"

Luke flipped through the transcripts, then said, "Yes."

"Please turn to page three."

Luke flipped to page three.

"Please find the fifth paragraph from the top. Let me know when you've found the spot."

Luke used his finger to find the spot. "I think I got it."

DA Perkins peered over the witness box, checking that Luke had the right spot. "Perfect. According to the transcripts, Detective Armstrong asked you the following question." Perkins paused for effect. "'Do you really believe Officer Lambert would've killed you if you would've dropped that baton? A decorated officer who has never shot anyone?' Your response is right below. Could you please read your response?"

Luke spoke barely above a whisper. "It was a mistake. I'm so sorry."

Perkins tilted his ear to Luke. "I couldn't hear you. Please speak up.

Louder, Luke read the transcript. "It was a mistake. I'm so sorry."

Perkins checked the jury, then said to Luke, "Detective Armstrong then said, 'You didn't answer my question. Do you believe Officer Lambert would've killed you if you didn't hit him in the head and kill him first?' Please read your response."

Through gritted teeth, Luke said, "No."

Perkins glanced at the jury, giving them a look, before returning to his podium, and addressing Luke again. "I'm confused. A few minutes ago, when Ms. Walters asked if you were afraid for your life, you said yes, but immediately after the incident occurred with Officer Lambert, you admitted that you were *not* in mortal danger. Which is it, Mr. Archer? Are you lying now or were you lying then?"

"Objection. Argumentative," Gina said.

"Overruled." Judge Malone turned to Luke and said, "Answer the question, Mr. Archer."

"I was feeling guilty right after it happened. Detective Armstrong used my faith against me. I wasn't thinking clearly. I *was* afraid for my life."

DA Perkins frowned. "Are we supposed to believe that your initial answers immediately after the incident were false, but *now* they're truthful, after you've figured out that you might go to prison for life?"

Gina stood from her seat. "*Objection.* Argumentative."

"Sustained," Judge Malone said.

"Withdrawn. I'm done with this witness," Perkins said.

***

After lunch, Gina Walters called the final witness for the defense.

Hushed whispers came from the audience, as Elizabeth Lambert took the stand. The judge administered her oath.

Gina Walters stood behind the podium. "Good afternoon, Mrs. Lambert."

Lizzie nodded, looking smart in a dark skirt suit. "Good afternoon."

Gina took a deep breath and asked, "Did you ever fear for your life when your late husband abused you?"

The courtroom erupted. Audible shouts came from the audience.

DA Perkins sprang from his seat. "Objection. *Prejudicial.*"

Judge Malone banged his gavel. "Order. Order in the court."

Lizzie sat with her head held high, despite the turmoil around her.

The courtroom quieted after a long moment.

Judge Malone glowered at Gina. "Does this witness have testimony that's pertinent to this case?"

With a straight face, Gina said, "Her testimony speaks to the character—"

"Don't even think about it, Ms. Walters. The victim isn't on trial." Judge Malone stabbed his finger at Gina. "I'm extremely disappointed that you'd try to pull a stunt like this in my courtroom. I should hold you in contempt."

CHAPTER 74: LUKE AND CLOSING STATEMENTS

"The law is on our side," DA Alex Perkins said, standing in front of the jury. "We have video evidence corroborating the facts of this case." Perkins half turned and gestured to Luke, sitting at the defense table. "In addition, the defendant admitted to killing Officer Bradley Lambert, a decorated police officer, with a wife and two children." Perkins faced the jury again. "We have forensic evidence that verifies the facts. The defendant's fingerprints were on the murder weapon. Officer Lambert's blood was on the end of the murder weapon, his own baton, the baton that was violently snatched from him by the defendant. The medical examiner determined that the cause of death was blunt force trauma." Perkins gestured to Luke again. "Blunt force trauma from the blow delivered by the defendant."

DA Perkins surveyed the jurors. "There is no question that the defendant killed Officer Bradley Lambert. Even the defense acknowledges this fact. The central question is whether or not the defendant killed Officer Lambert in self-defense. This is where you *must* follow the law. The defense is obscuring facts, playing on your emotions. Don't fall for the theatrics. You must follow the facts. You must follow the law." Perkins paced along the jury box. "When the defendant exited Mason's Farm & Feed on that morning of May seventh, he had no idea why Officer Lambert was fighting with Curtis Mays. The defendant had no idea that Curtis Mays had spat on Officer Lambert and resisted arrest. Still, the defendant interfered with the official duties of a peace officer by assaulting Officer Lambert."

Perkins stopped pacing and nodded to the jury, letting that point marinate for a few seconds. "After the defendant assaulted Officer Lambert, what did Bradley Lambert do? Did he immediately attack the defendant?" Perkins shook his head. "No. No, he did not. He told the defendant to get on the ground." Perkins held up two fingers. "Not once, but *twice*."

Luke's heart thumped in his chest, remembering the events of May seventh as DA Perkins recounted them. *I should've done what I was told.* Luke knew Officer Lambert had told him to get on the ground, but, at the time, he was fearful of a deadly beating, should he assume the same prone position Curtis had.

Perkins continued. "All the defendant had to do was lay on the ground, and Officer Lambert would still be alive. But the defendant didn't. The defendant resisted a lawful arrest with murderous force. Those are the facts. Facts that are verified with video evidence, forensics, and a full confession by the defendant." DA Perkins took a deep breath and rested his hands on the jury box. "This is the most important case I've ever seen in my twenty-two years as the district attorney in Carville. It has far-reaching implications, not just for Carville but for the entire commonwealth of Pennsylvania, maybe for the entire United States."

Perkins paused, letting his point sink in. "If you fail to follow the law, if you fail to follow the truth, if you fail to convict the defendant of first-degree murder of a law enforcement officer, you will be endangering every single police officer in Pennsylvania. You will open the door for violent criminals to resist arrest, to kill police officers, and all in the name of *evil* disguised as self-defense." Perkins made eye contact with each juror. "Follow the law. Follow the facts. Do the right thing. Thank you."

Perkins walked back to the prosecution table.

Someone in the audience clapped for a second, stopping after the room didn't join him or her. But Luke thought the room wanted to clap and cheer—like the home team had just scored the winning touchdown.

Luke stared at the tabletop before him. *I'm finished.*

Gina nudged Luke and whispered, "Chin up. The jury's watching your body language."

Luke raised his gaze.

Gina stood and marched to the jury box. "Good morning."

A few jurors mouthed, *Good morning.*

The foreman said, "Mornin'."

Gina scanned the jury. "I want you all to imagine that you go grocery shopping on a weekday morning. As you're leaving the grocery store, you see a man beating another man with a metal pipe. The man being beaten isn't moving. The parking lot is empty. There's nobody to call for help. Even a call to the police would take too long. If you delay, that unconscious man will likely die. What would you do?" Gina let the jurors consider the question for a few seconds. "I can't speak for you, but, if I'm honest with myself, I would likely run for help or call the police, and—in that circumstance—the unconscious man would likely die, and the perpetrator would likely run free. I don't have the courage to put my own safety at risk for the life of another human being, especially someone I've never met. Do you?"

Gina gestured to the jury. "Let's imagine you *do* have the courage to intervene. To save that unconscious man from certain death. Let's imagine you push the perpetrator to the ground, and then that perpetrator turns his metal pipe on *you*. Do you let the perpetrator beat you to death in the same manner you'd just witnessed? Or do you defend yourself?" Gina rested her hands on the jury box. "Imagine that you have the courage to fight for your own life too. In doing so, you take that metal pipe from the perpetrator and hit him over the head, not to kill him, but to protect yourself. Imagine, you connect with his temple, killing him."

Gina took a deep breath and half turned, gesturing to Luke at the defense table. "Make no mistake. That's exactly what happened to Luke Archer. The only reason we're here is the man with the metal baton was wearing a police uniform. If Officer Lambert was simply a civilian, Luke Archer *never* would've been prosecuted." Gina faced the jury again. "We are all equal under the law, aren't we?" Gina thrummed her fingers on the jury box. "Aren't we?"

Two jurors nodded in agreement.

The jury foreman stared at Gina, expressionless.

Gina continued. "The commonwealth says that they have the truth and the law is on their side, but that's not true. Officer Lambert had *no* right to beat Curtis Mays for spitting on the ground. From the bodycam footage, you can clearly see that Curtis turned his head away from Officer Lambert to spit. Luke Archer had *every* right to interfere with an unlawful arrest. Luke Archer had every right to defend himself against an out-of-control officer who had been beating Curtis Mays to death."

Gina held out her hands. "Why on Earth should Luke Archer obey Officer Lambert's commands to get on the ground? Luke had just witnessed Curtis being beaten unconscious in that very position." Gina looked at the jury foreman. "Would you lay on the ground in that situation? Would you trust that Officer Lambert would simply handcuff you after what you had just witnessed?"

The jury foreman didn't appear to react, his face difficult to read under his bushy beard.

Gina's gaze moved to the next juror. As she spoke, she stopped for a beat at each one. "If you convict Luke Archer, you must believe that the police have a legal right to beat us for simply spitting near them. You must believe that the police have the power to do with us as they please. You must believe that we must submit to assault and possibly murder by the police, regardless of the circumstances. You must believe we have *no* right to life or liberty."

CHAPTER 75: LIZZIE AND HEALING

Lizzie sat at her kitchen table, browsing Penn State World Campus on her laptop. They had an online nursing program she was interested in. It cost $70K, but she had money from Brad's insurance and death benefits, and she was certain she qualified for financial aid. Her mind drifted to the trial, which would be over soon. Closing statements were scheduled for that Friday morning. She wore her skirt suit because she'd planned to go, but then she'd changed her mind. Either outcome would hurt. Lizzie checked the time on her laptop—*10:06 a.m. It might already be over.*

The doorbell chimed. Lizzie walked to the front door and checked the sidelight window, seeing a woman holding a plastic case. The young woman looked familiar. Then it hit her. Lizzie had seen her sitting next to Mary Archer at the trial.

Lizzie opened the door, the cold air rushing inside, and asked, "May I help you?"

The young woman smiled. "Hi. I'm Tisha Hicks. I run a nonprofit called Justice for Carville."

Lizzie narrowed her eyes. "You're with Curtis Mays."

Tisha smiled again. "Yes. He's my partner—"

"What do you want?"

"I want you to tell your story."

Lizzie crossed her arms over her chest. "What story?"

"The story you didn't get to tell at trial."

Lizzie pursed her lips, standing in the cold open doorway.

Tisha gestured with her free hand. "Thank you by the way."

Lizzie dropped her arms to her side. "For what?"

"For having the courage to speak out at the trial."

"It didn't do any good."

"That's why I'm here."

186

Lizzie invited Tisha inside. Tisha explained their documentary and that she just wanted Lizzie to say what she would've said at trial. After some coaxing, Lizzie agreed to tell her story.

Lizzie sat on her living room couch. Tisha set up the camera, facing Lizzie.

Standing behind the camera, Tisha said, "You can begin whenever you're ready."

Lizzie took a deep breath. "My husband was Officer Brad Lambert. I loved my husband dearly. I have two wonderful children because of him. He was a great father, and, for the most part, he was a good husband. It's just ..." Lizzie looked down. "He was physically and mentally abusive to me." She went quiet for several seconds. Then she raised her gaze. "I think he experienced too much violence throughout his lifetime. He didn't have the right coping skills or something. His father had been very abusive to him when he was a child. He experienced things in Iraq that no human being should experience."

Lizzie sighed and shook her head. "On the day he died, he told me that he wanted to take another job. A private security job. He was tired of all the negativity involved with police work. He didn't like the ticket quotas. He didn't like giving people tickets for minor offenses, but it was part of the job. I discouraged him though." Lizzie swallowed hard, tears filling her eyes. "The security job didn't pay enough to cover our bills. I told him that we needed the money, and he told me not to worry, that he'd suck it up."

Lizzie wiped the corners of her eyes. "What happened wasn't all his fault. It was partly mine. I wish I could go back to that day and tell him to quit right then and there, that the money didn't matter. Of course, that's not what happened. He went to work, and he beat Curtis Mays unconscious. Luke Archer intervened, but that didn't stop him from going after Mr. Archer."

From behind the camera, Tisha asked, "Did you see the bodycam footage of the altercation between Curtis Mays, Luke Archer, and your husband?"

Lizzie nodded. "I did."

"Based on what you saw, and your personal experience, do you think your husband would've killed Curtis Mays if Luke Archer hadn't intervened?"

Lizzie let out a heavy breath. "Yes."

"If Luke Archer hadn't defended *himself*, do you think your husband would've killed him?"

Lizzie stared at the coffee table for a long moment. Then she peered into the camera and said, "Yes."

CHAPTER 76: MARY AND THE VERDICT

Late on Friday afternoon, the jury was back from deliberations. Mary sat sandwiched between Curtis and his father, Leonard.

The jury foreman said to the judge, "We can't reach a verdict."

Judge Malone scowled at the jury. "I'm going to dismiss you for the weekend. You are *not* to watch television, use the internet, or read the newspaper. You are *not* to discuss this case with anyone. I expect that you'll reflect on the trial individually, and when you come back on Monday, you'll resume deliberations. I fully expect that you *will* reach a unanimous verdict." Judge Malone banged his gavel. "Court is adjourned."

The courtroom audience stood and erupted in a cacophony of voices. Mary, Curtis, and Leonard stood too.

Luke was escorted from the courtroom by two deputies. He gave Mary a small smile on his way out. Mary smiled back, following Luke with her gaze, until he had exited the courtroom near the judge's bench.

Mary turned to Curtis, as they waited for the crowd to exit the courtroom. "What does this mean?"

"It's a hung jury, meaning that the jurors don't all agree," Curtis said. "They need a unanimous decision, one way or the other, to acquit or to convict."

"What happens if they can't agree?"

"They might retry the case."

Mary's shoulders slumped.

"Don't worry. This is good. I have a feeling the jury will come back from the weekend with a better perspective."

CHAPTER 77: LIZZIE AND THE DOCUMENTARY

Lizzie pushed into Brian's bedroom. Her son sat on his bed, tapping on his iPad.

"Time for bed, honey," Lizzie said, approaching the bedside.

Brian paused his game. "Aw, come on, Mom. It's Saturday night."

"I don't want you off your schedule. You'll be a zombie at school on Monday."

"I'm not tired yet."

"You don't have to go to sleep. You can read until you get sleepy but no devices." Lizzie took his iPad and kissed him on the forehead. "You have so many good books."

Brian nodded. "Okay."

Lizzie hugged him and said, "I love you."

When they separated, he said, "Love you too, Mom."

Lizzie smiled and left the room, as Brian searched his bookcase for a bedtime story. She went to Emma's room, next door. Emma played with her Barbie dreamhouse, wearing her princess pajamas.

"Time for bed, honey," Lizzie said.

Emma turned from her Barbies to Lizzie. "Will you read me a story?"

"Just one." Lizzie gestured to her little bookcase. "Pick one."

Emma picked *Margaret's Unicorn* from her bookshelf and settled into her bed with Lizzie. Emma listened intently, focused on the images, as Lizzie read the story. Emma read along with certain parts, practicing her new skill.

At the conclusion of the story, Emma said, "I wish I had a unicorn."

"So do I," Lizzie replied.

"Do you think they have unicorns in heaven?"

"I don't know. I hope so."

"Me too. I think Daddy needs a friend."

Lizzie hugged her daughter and kissed the crown of her head. Lizzie's voice quivered, as she spoke. "I think he does too."

After being coerced into another story, Lizzie tucked Emma into bed and kissed her good night. Lizzie went into her bedroom and climbed into bed. She grabbed her phone and scrolled through her Facebook feed, feeling a little hypocritical for being on *her* device after taking Brian's.

At the top of her feed was a video entitled, *Justice for Carville*. It had already been viewed over half-a-million times. The description mentioned her by name, along with Fred Mason. She scrolled through the comments.

Gayle Wilson: The Carville cops are seriously corrupt.

Adam Brossman: I've known Fred Mason for thirty-years. He's telling the truth about Chief Rhodes. Rhodes is a POS.

Ray Ulysses: FREE LUKE

Trevor Franklin: Shame on you, Carville County!!!

Pat Hempstead: My sister lives there. She nearly lost her home because of stupid code violations. I mean, really stupid. Like having her bushes growing into the street by like an inch. And nobody even drives through there. She lives on a dead-end cul-de-sac. She would prune them, and, as soon as the hedge would grow back, she'd get another fine.

Gloria Rivera: We are all tired of the tickets for NOTHING. Carville County is a disgrace.

Jodie Harris: Chief Rhodes should be in prison

Will Simons: FREE LUKE

Kristin Simmons: I feel bad for Elizabeth Lambert. She is brave for coming forward.

CHAPTER 78: CURTIS AND THE MARCH

By the end of the day on Monday, the jury was still deadlocked, but the judge was resolute.

Judge Malone had said, "You will resume deliberations tomorrow morning. I expect you to come to an agreement."

Over the weekend, Curtis and Tisha's documentary had gone viral, with over two million views spread across Facebook and YouTube. To capitalize on their success, they had planned a Monday night march from a half-empty strip mall to the courthouse downtown.

Curtis parked his father's truck in the back of the strip mall parking lot. Tisha and Mary sat next to him on the bench seat. Abby was with a trusted neighbor. The lot was half full of cars, their exhaust fumes condensing in the cold air. The clock in the truck read 6:17 p.m. They were forty-three minutes early.

"Are all these people here for us?" Mary asked.

Curtis scanned the dark storefronts. "The stores are closed. Most of them close at six."

"A lot of these license plates are out of state," Tisha said.

Curtis squinted through the windshield, spotting many New York, New Jersey, Maryland, and Virginia plates. "Not sure if that's a good thing."

Mary glanced over her shoulder at the homemade signs stacked in the truck bed. "We should've made more signs."

Over the next forty-three minutes, the parking lot overfilled, with many people parking on the shoulder and walking to the strip mall. Curtis, Tisha, and Mary greeted the protesters and handed out homemade signs that read Justice for Carville, Free Luke, and Chief Rhodes for Prison. Many protesters brought Black Lives Matter signs, although Curtis hadn't heard from any official BLM representative.

Twenty to thirty people gathered in the back corner of the lot. They were dressed in all black, their faces covered like bandits. *Antifa.*

At exactly 7:00 p.m., Curtis stood in the middle of the crowd, speaking on his bullhorn. "Thank you all for coming out."

Cheers came from the crowd.

Curtis waited for the cheers to subside. "We're going to walk from here to the courthouse, which is about a fifteen-minute walk. When we get there, Mary Archer will make a speech on the courthouse steps. This demonstration is meant to be peaceful. Please do not litter or destroy any property. And absolutely no violence under any circumstances. We are trying to win the hearts and minds of the citizens of Carville. Any violence or vandalism undermines our goal." Curtis paused for a beat, emphasizing his final point. "All right. Let's go. Everyone fall in line behind the banner."

Tisha organized the big banner that read Justice for Carville. Tisha and Mary held the banner, with several other protesters. Curtis walked in front, leading them toward the courthouse, keeping protesters behind the banner. Curtis estimated that one thousand people had come to march that night.

As they walked through the rowhouses of Carville, several black-clad protesters hit and kicked the cars as they passed, setting off alarms.

Curtis told Tisha to keep marching, and he ran toward the group of Antifa, speaking through his bullhorn. "What the hell are you doing?"

They stared at Curtis, silent, their faces covered.

Curtis gestured to the rowhouses. "These are the people we're trying to help. If you can't march peacefully, go the fuck home."

The black-clad protesters marched past Curtis, nudging him with their shoulders as they passed.

Curtis pushed one of them and said, "Back off."

Curtis returned to the front and led the protesters down Main Street. The crowd had grown in size since they'd left the strip mall. As they approached the courthouse, a small crowd was already there. In addition, police officers, holding shields and wearing riot gear, stood in a line across the front of the courthouse. The awaiting crowd was counterprotesting, holding Blue Lives Matter and Luke Archer, Cop Killer signs.

As they approached the courthouse steps, Antifa and the counterprotesters traded obscenities.

The crowds and onlookers coalesced into a throng of nearly two thousand people. Curtis and Tisha led Mary through the crowd to the top of the courthouse steps, just in front of the police officers.

Based on their experience, Curtis and Tisha had figured on a crowd of one hundred people, so they didn't have a podium or a microphone for Mary.

The crowd was too noisy to talk over, so Curtis gave her the mike attached to his bullhorn. "Just press the button on the side to talk."

Mary stood tight to Tisha and shook her head. "I don't think I can do this."

Curtis leaned toward Mary, the crowd getting louder. "What's wrong?"

"I can't do it."

"You didn't prepare a speech?"

"I did. I didn't think it would be so many people."

"It's okay. I'll do it. Maybe you can just thank them for coming at the end."

Mary nodded, looking at Curtis, then Tisha. "I'm sorry."

"You're fine. Don't worry about it," Curtis replied.

"It's okay," Tisha echoed.

Curtis faced the crowd. He spoke into the mike. "Thank you so much for coming out tonight and supporting Luke Archer and Justice for Carville."

The crowd cheered.

"I hope this brings awareness to the corruption in the Carville County government. For too long the residents of Carville have endured hardships brought about by excessive fines, excessive laws, and corruption perpetrated by the Carville County Police and government."

The crowd cheered louder. Signs shook. A glass bottle broke nearby. Then another. A fist fight broke out between Antifa and the counterprotesters. Then the crowd erupted, some people pushing their way out—some people pushing their way in. Both sides hurled trash back and forth. An errant bottle zipped past Curtis's head.

The riot police marched forward.

A police officer spoke into his bullhorn. "This is an illegal gathering. Please disperse, or you will be arrested."

More riot police came from the north on Main Street, pushing the crowd to the south, back the way they came. The riot police were supported by an armored personnel carrier, with policemen riding on the running boards. Antifa and the counterprotesters still fought, mostly with fists. Some of the trash was thrown at the police, their shields protecting them from glass bottles, rocks, and plastic water bottles weighted with water, urine, or gravel. Several protestors held their heads in the pandemonium, blood coming from their wounds.

"Let's get out of here," Curtis said to Tisha and Mary. Curtis took Tisha's hand.

Tisha took Mary's hand.

Curtis pushed through the crowd. People and bodies pushed against him. He held tight to Tisha's hand. They went with the current, the crowd moving away from the riot police.

As the riot police pushed the crowd south on Main Street, they echoed the same message with the speakers coming from the personnel carrier. "This is an illegal gathering. Please disperse, or you will be arrested."

As the crowd retreated, Antifa and many others smashed car windows and shop windows with crowbars. They also set fire to a Dumpster on wheels. A half-dozen young men pushed the blazing Dumpster toward a gas station. They were having trouble with the slight incline, but, if they crested the hill, it was downhill to the gas station. Curtis let go of Tisha's hand and ran to the Dumpster.

Just before they crested the hill, Curtis slammed into the Dumpster, halting their progress.

Two black-clad young men grabbed Curtis by his collar, pulling him away from the Dumpster. Curtis resisted. One of them punched Curtis in the face, the blow weak, glancing off his face. Curtis turned and swung, connecting with the young man's jaw, causing him to fall awkwardly. The other black-clad man stepped back, no longer interested in fighting.

Curtis shouted at the young men, "You don't even live here! Go the fuck home."

A man behind the Dumpster stepped around the others to Curtis. His face was uncovered, partially lit by the fire. He said, "*I live here.*" Daryl brandished his handgun. "Get the fuck outta the way, nigga."

Curtis showed his palms and stepped back, away from the Dumpster. "Come on, Daryl. Don't do this."

Daryl nodded to the others. "Go on. Push, motherfuckers."

"This is our home."

Daryl shook his head. "That's some bullshit."

The young men grunted and pushed, cresting the hill, as Daryl held Curtis at gunpoint. Once the Dumpster was over the hill, it picked up speed, racing to the gas station. At first the young men guided the Dumpster, but then it got away from them, still rumbling toward the gas station. The fiery Dumpster collided with the auto-diesel pump. The black-clad young men cheered.

Their cheers dissipated as nothing happened, the Dumpster fire crackling in the cold air. Two of the young men sauntered over to give the Dumpster another push. Sparks from the Dumpster fire floated to the concrete, most failing to ignite. But one started a small fire. The fire spread toward the pump.

"Wait!" Curtis shouted.

The explosion sent Curtis to the ground, and the crowd stampeding again. Curtis watched the two young men writhe among the flames, until their bodies were still.

Amid the chaos, Curtis heard his name. It sounded like Tisha. Curtis stood and turned to Tisha's voice, but Daryl still held him at gunpoint.

"Where the fuck you think you're goin'?" Daryl asked.

Curtis heard his name again. "Go ahead and shoot me." Curtis ran toward Tisha, never looking back.

Daryl never fired.

Curtis fought his way through the crowd, like a salmon swimming against the current, following Tisha's voice. He found Tisha in the middle of Main Street, kneeling over Mary's petite frame, blood coming from Mary's head, her jacket dirty with shoe and boot prints. She appeared to be unconscious.

Tisha looked up at Curtis, her eyes red, and her face tear-streaked. "Someone knocked her over, and they just stomped her."

"We have to get her to a hospital," Curtis said, kneeling next to Tisha. Curtis reached under Mary and lifted her like a newlywed might carry his betrothed over the threshold.

Tisha ran toward the riot police, her hands waving in the air. Curtis rushed after Tisha, carrying Mary, trying not to jostle her too much. Tisha slowed, as she approached the line of riot police.

A policeman's voice came over the loudspeaker. "This is an unlawful gathering. Please disperse, or you will be arrested."

Tisha gestured to Curtis, hurrying toward them with Mary jostling in his arms, and said to the line of riot police, "She needs medical attention! Please help!"

As Curtis rumbled toward the police, he worried that they'd be mistaken as a threat somehow.

The riot police kept their line tight.

Curtis slowed as he neared the police line, his breath elevated, still holding Mary.

"What are you doing?" Tisha shouted, gesturing to Mary again. "Help her!"

Three police officers dropped their shields and ran to Curtis and Mary.

CHAPTER 79: LUKE AND THE VERDICT

Luke glanced over his shoulder, the courtroom audience packed with police officers, but no Mary or Curtis. More than a few police officers glared at him. He heard two deputies talking about the riot in Carville last night. A gas station had exploded, and several cars were set on fire. He didn't think Mary would've been there, but the fact that she and Curtis weren't at trial that morning terrified him.

Luke faced forward and addressed Gina, sitting to his right at the defense table. "Can you call her again?"

Gina turned from her legal pad, just as the jury filed into the courtroom. They had deliberated for less than an hour. She whispered, "I'm sure she's fine. She's probably in the hall. The courtroom filled up pretty early this morning."

His eyes bulged, and he spoke rapidly. "She wouldn't miss this. It might be the last time I see her outside of prison."

"Have faith."

Luke clasped his hands together. *Please, God, wherever my family is, keep them safe. And please give me the justice I deserve. Whatever the outcome, I have faith in You.*

The jury foreman handed a folder to the bailiff, who handed the folder to the judge. Judge Malone opened the folder and read the form for a minute, then handed it back to the bailiff. The bailiff handed the form back to the foreman and gave him a few muted instructions.

"Luke Archer, please stand for the reading of the verdict," Judge Malone said.

Gina Walters stood, then Luke, his legs like Jell-O.

"You may read the verdict," Malone said.

The jury foreman stood in front of his seat on the jury, holding the folder open. He read from the form without emotion. "For the charge of murder in the first degree of a law enforcement officer, we find the defendant ..."

CHAPTER 80: MARY AND THE END

The gas station exploded. Someone knocked Mary to the macadam, separating her from Tisha. People screamed and ran, tripping over each other, and stepping on each other. Anything to escape danger. Mary tried to rise, but a heavy boot stepped on her chest. Another kicked her head, knocking her unconscious. Mary watched herself from above, the crowd swallowing her whole. Mary fought to get up, but her body wouldn't move.

A faint voice came from the night sky.

Her body. The crowd. The gas station inferno. It all faded to black.

The voice grew louder.

The black turned to gray. A dark blob-like figure stood over her.

Her eyes fluttered.

The blob sharpened into a person-shape. Her mind was fuzzy, like she was there and not there at the same time. Mary tried to raise her head, but pain stopped her. Cool oxygen flowed into her nose from some sort of tube. She lay on her back, squinting into the light, the person coming into focus.

Luke hovered over her, his eyes bloodshot. "Mary? Are you okay?"

Mary blinked several times and spoke in a raspy voice. "My head hurts. My chest."

Luke took Mary's hand. "Just relax. I called the nurse."

Mary scanned the hospital room. "Where's Abby?"

"Tisha and Curtis have her in the waiting room."

"What happened?"

"Somebody kicked you in the head. They stepped on you. The doctor said you have swelling in your brain, but she thought you'd wake up as soon as the swelling went down. You have a concussion. Your body's bruised, but she said there were no internal injuries."

"*No.* What happened with the trial?"

Luke smiled. "It was a miracle."

Epilogue: Luke, Four Months Later

Luke kneeled in the greenhouse, cutting the last of the kale, and tossing the blue leaves into his bin. He hummed to himself, immersed in the repetitive work. The greenhouse door opened. Mary led a large man his way. She had the tiniest of baby bumps. Luke stood from his work and brushed the compost off his canvas pants.

Mary smiled and gestured to the Paul Bunyan look-alike. "I'm assuming you remember this face?"

The man held out his hand. "Randy Lassiter."

Luke shook hands with the former jury foreman.

"I'll leave you two to talk." Mary exited the greenhouse.

"I'm sorry for droppin' in on you outta the blue like this," Randy said. "I thought about emailin' your business, but I didn't want any record of this. Even with Chief Rhodes resigning, I still don't trust the Carville police. Maybe I'm bein' paranoid, but you never know around here."

Luke nodded. "I understand. What can I do for you?"

Randy slipped his hands into the pockets of his bib overalls. "I wanted to talk to you right after the trial, but I didn't want people thinkin' we were friends, sayin' that was why you were acquitted."

Luke nodded again. "What did you want to talk about?"

"I'm a believer, like you, and I figure what you did must weigh heavy on you."

Luke exhaled. "I wish it never happened."

"I wanted to tell you face-to-face, for what it's worth, I think you did the right thing."

"Thanks." Luke paused for an instant. "I'm still surprised. I thought I'd be convicted."

"Well, we had two sticklers on the jury, who thought you should go to prison. They kept citin' the law, and the rest of us kept talkin' about what was right. That was why we were deadlocked."

"Why did they change their mind?"

Randy shrugged. "Don't know. They didn't say. Maybe they saw that documentary. We weren't supposed to watch the news or go on the internet, but I doubt anybody followed that."

"That makes sense," Luke replied.

"Or maybe they finally figured out that the law and morality ain't the same thing."

If you enjoyed this novel, ... you'll love Cesspool.

Would you become a criminal to do the right thing?

Disgraced teacher, James Fisher, moved to a backwoods town, content to live his life in solitude. He was awakened from his apathy by a small girl with a big problem. James suspected Brittany was being abused and exploited by his neighbor. He called the police but soon realized his mistake, as the neighbor was related to the chief of police.

Most would've looked the other way. Getting involved placed James squarely in the crosshairs of the local police. James lacked the brawn or the connections to save himself, much less Brittany. The police held all the power, and they knew it. But that was also their weakness. They underestimated what the mild-mannered teacher and the young runaway would do for justice.

Buy *Cesspool* today if you enjoy vigilante justice page-turners with a side of underdog.

Adult language and content.

<u>What Readers Are Saying</u>

"Wow. Just wow. This book was amazing. Every chapter, every page had me thinking about ideas, philosophies, current events, history in a different way." - Elaine ★★★★★

"The writing is excellent, the pace quick, the characters and dialog believable. An excellent read." - Dusty Sharp, Author of the Austin Conrad Series ★★★★★

"I have enjoyed this author before, but this is his best yet. If you want a story that will keep you reading, this is it. The story, the characters, and the cunning displayed by the hero is some of the best fiction I've had the pleasure to read. Do yourself a favor and pick up this book. You won't lay it down until the end." - Patrick R. ★★★★★

"Wow! This was one of the best books I've read in a while. Twists, turns, and unexpected events in every chapter. What a movie this would make." – Kindle Customer ★★★★★

"This book was incredible! I read it in three days—the entire story is a whirlwind of fantastic characters, a perfect constancy of ups and downs throughout." - Rae L. ★★★★★

FOR THE READER

Dear Reader,

I'm thrilled that you took precious time out of your life to read my novel. Thank you! I hope you found it entertaining, engaging, and thought-provoking. If so, please consider writing a positive review on Amazon and Goodreads. Five-star reviews have a huge impact on future sales. The review doesn't need to be long and detailed if you're more of a reader than a writer. As an author and a small businessman, competing against the big publishers, I greatly appreciate every reader, every review, and every referral.

If you're interested in receiving two of my novels for free and/or reading my other titles for free or discounted, go to the following link: http://www.PhilWBooks.com. You're probably thinking, *What's the catch?* There is no catch.

If you want to contact me, don't be bashful. I can be found at Phil@PhilWBooks.com. I do my best to respond to all emails.

Sincerely,

Phil M. Williams

GRATITUDE

I'd like to thank my wife for being my first reader, sounding board, and cheerleader. Without her support and unwavering belief in my skill as an author, I'm not sure I would have embarked on this career. I love you, Denise.

I'd also like to thank my editors. My developmental editor, Caroline Smailes, did a fantastic job finding the holes in my plot and suggesting remedies. As always, my line editor, Denise Barker (not to be confused with my wife, Denise Williams), did a fantastic job making sure the manuscript was error-free. I love her comments and feedback.

Thank you to my good friend Barry for his invaluable legal knowledge. Any mistakes regarding the legal system were mine alone. And lastly, thank you as always to my mother-in-law, Joy, one of the best nurses on this planet. She is always gracious with her time and extremely knowledgeable about all things medical.

Thank you to my beta readers, Sue, Saundra, Ray, and Ann. They're my last defense against the dreaded typo. And thank you to you, the reader. Without you, I wouldn't have a career. As long as you keep reading, I'll keep writing.

www.ingramcontent.com/pod-product-compliance
Lightning Source LLC
Chambersburg PA
CBHW020422180626
46812CB00003B/1106